A Talk on the Wild Side

imaginary interviews
with unlikely sources of wisdom

by

OLGA SHEEAN

Published by InsideOut Media

CONTENTS

INFODUCTION

A TALK ON THE WILD SIDE is a motley assortment of irreverent, humorous, rabble-rousing, off-the-wall, spontaneous, subversive and sometimes downright annoying conversations with animate and inanimate subjects, many of whose voices would otherwise never be heard. This book is a work of fiction, and most of these interviews took place inside my head (although a few occurred when I was clearly not in my right mind). Any resemblance to statements that certain entities might or might not have uttered is entirely unintentional, although coincidences do happen...

Humour, creativity and playfulness are some of our most powerful human traits, connecting and uniting us in universal ways. They can also be deeply transformative and enlightening, lifting us out of the analysis and concerns that tend to dominate our lives. Laughing ourselves silly is also extremely good for our health, not to mention our sex life.

Each interview in this book has its own special theme—but I'll leave it to you to figure out what that might be (although I've given you some clues, in brackets, after the chapter headings). The goal of this book is to encourage us all to laugh at ourselves, while also seeing the wisdom and wonder in objects with which we might not normally, um, converse. It will also hopefully help us to see the value of questioning everything—especially the kinds of questions that we ask, which are often as pre-determined and predictable as our answers, due to our firmly embedded thoughts and beliefs. Only by truly questioning everything—yes, even that thought you just had—can we ever begin to know our own minds. Even then, we may never be entirely free of all the beliefs we absorbed from our early caregivers, back when we were hungry little sponges, focused on being fed and cared for. Nor can we ever be truly objective or detached about the religious beliefs that pervade all aspects of society.

Read this with an open mind, a playful spirit ...and a bucketful of popcorn—to remind yourself that it is, after all, intended to entertain you and help you to see the funny side of life, as well as the painful ironies that result when we take ourselves too seriously.

And remember: if *you* don't laugh at yourself, someone else will.

1. Interview with my subconscious
[its purpose]

OS: Hey, good to connect, finally. I'd love to talk about what goes on behind the scenes—sort of get the inside scoop on me. I mean, you're responsible for all the patterns in my life and it would be good to get some firsthand info about what's really going on.

Subconscious: No comment.

OS: Look, I know you don't normally do this; you work under cover—I get that—but could we at least talk about some of the issues I've had?

Subconscious: No.

OS: Aren't you supposed to be on my side, bringing me whatever I need to reach my potential and be fulfilled?

Subconscious: Absolutely not.

OS: Oh, come on. That's precisely what you do. I've seen it happen too many times for you to fob me off like that.

Subconscious: No.

OS: Well, what the heck *is* your job, then?

Subconscious: None of your business.

OS: What? How can it be none of my business? You're there to serve me! You're MY subconscious. Don't I have any say in this at all?

Subconscious: If you did, you wouldn't need a subconscious.

OS: What's *that* supposed to mean?

Subconscious: Think about it—with that non-stop-thinking conscious mind of yours.

OS: So you're saying I need a subconscious that does things behind my back, sets me up for all kinds of challenging, painful, formative experiences, throws me the odd insight, if I'm really persistent, but never lets me see the full picture so that I can understand what's really going on. That's your glorious purpose in my life?

Subconscious: Yep.

OS: But why? I don't get it. Why—

Subconscious: Think.

OS: It's subversive. You're acting as if you're there to bring down the very organism you're meant to serve. It doesn't make sense.

Subconscious: Subversive is good.

OS: But wh—

Subconscious: Think.

OS: Aaarrrhh. I hate you already. Is that part of your brief too? Okay, okay... Let's see... Well, if I can't get to the deeper reasons for what's going on in my life, I'm forced to have certain painful experiences... Sounds like normal life, for most people. How's that any different to not having you around at all?

Subconscious: Keep going. You give up far too easily.

OS: And you're a manipulative, underhanded, sneaky, double-crossing artful dodger.

Subconscious: Ah, now you're getting warmer.

OS: You stay hidden and inaccessible so that... what? So I get no easy answers? So I spend half my life getting things wrong—

Subconscious: Well, a little more than half, actually...

OS: Okay, you can add mean and spiteful to the list of your wonderful qualities.

Subconscious: Not mean, just literal—which is part of what makes me so reliable. Keep going.

OS: Reliable?? You're about as reliable as an e-mail from Nigeria.

Subconscious: Try to stay focused.

OS: You stay hidden and inaccessible so that... I look everywhere else but there. It's like trying to communicate with God, which no one can touch or prove or tangibly define. In fact, now that I think about it, that's it, isn't it? You have all those same attributes and I could say all the same things about you that people say about God—"*Oh, how could God let these bad things happen to me? What kind of God would* do *this?*" They blame God when things go wrong, and pray to him when they're in a bind. They try to negotiate, make deals. They use God to explain away things they can't explain—any more than they can access or explain their own subconscious minds. God's the fall guy, the dumping ground for whatever goes wrong; he's the higher authority we invoke if people don't take us seriously. We use him in all kinds of distorted ways because we have no idea of who/what he really is—because we have no idea of who/what *we* really are. He's ethereal, nebulous, something we can sometimes sense but never really capture. Just like you, right?

Subconscious: Oh, are we still having a conversation? I thought you were talking to yourself.

OS: I *am* talking to myself. You're it, remember?

Subconscious: If you say so.

OS: Well, did I get that right? You're the god in me that I must define through my own personal experience and that I must ultimately come back to, once I've seen through all the external projections of God—all those religious beliefs that try to pull me off course; you're the creative force that pushes me to explore my unlimited self and to realize that I have all those creative abilities too; and you're that unseen power that refuses to communicate directly or to explain itself, precisely so that I'm left to find all the answers on my own, without any reassurances from you, and to realize that I am god, too. Right? Hey, am I right or am I right? Hello? Anybody there...?

2. Interview with a newborn baby, Day 1
[programming/religion]

Newborn: What are *you* staring at?

OS: Me? I was just admiring you lying there, looking so innocent.

Newborn: Mmmm… You don't feel like mummy material. What are you doing here?

OS: I'm waiting for a friend. She's a nurse in the neonatal unit and she said I could do some baby-watching while I was waiting.

Newborn: And you were staring at me because…?

OS: You looked so alert and switched on.

Newborn: Gotta stay alert or I could end up with the wrong name tag or medication. Not that I could really do much about it. Actually, it might be kind of interesting to get switched.

OS: You think so?

Newborn: Nah. It wouldn't change much, really.

OS: Surely it would change everything.

Newborn: It's all the same stuff, whether I'm born into an English family, a North American one or an East Indian one. We all get the same kind of programming. Same pyjamas, just different colours.

OS: What do you mean?

Newborn: I've been communing with that little baldie over there—the one with the coffee-coloured skin—and he says he's getting all the same stuff from his Hindu parents.

OS: What kind of stuff?

Newborn: Well, for him, a nappy-load of prayers and rituals, before he even gets here—at conception, halfway through pregnancy, and then more stuff when he's born, when he's named, when he has his first mouthful of solid food, and then he'll have to take some vows before he starts school and he'll be told all about his responsibility to continue the Hindu traditions…I feel colicky just thinking about it. And people wonder why we get SIDS! They call it Sudden Infant Death Syndrome, but it's more like Suffocating Infant Down-Sizing.

OS: And for you? What religion are you?

Newborn: I'm not a religion! I'm a person, my own pristine self—for another few months, anyway. After that…

OS: Oh, don't cry. I'm sorry I upset you.

Newborn: You didn't. I'm only turning on the tears because it's almost feeding time here at the zoo, and they expect me to cry every three hours. Hang on a sec… *waa, waa, waa*. There. They just need to know my lungs are working okay. Now we've got about another 15 minutes before I have to turn it on full blast.

OS: That's a relief. So…what kind of stuff is going on with your parents?

Newborn: They're all worked up about when I should be baptized, which fancy school I must go to, who the godparents should be… Stifling stuff. And they can't even decide what to call me.

OS: They haven't chosen a name yet?

Newborn: Nope. He wants Sandro, because he's half Italian, but she wants Rory, after her great-great-great-uncle's Irish half-wit half-brother. My working title is Sandry, while they sort out a longer-term truce. Personally, I think *Sandwich* would be more appropriate.

OS: Oh, dear. Sounds as if things have got off to a rather shaky start. What would you like to be called?

Newborn: Veda.

OS: Nice. Very unusual. What does it mean?

Newborn: It's Turkish for farewell, as in: adios, bye-bye, I'm outta here, beam me up, Scottie.

OS: Oh. I see. You don't really want to be here.

Newborn: I'm a fix-it baby.

OS: A what?

Newborn: They think that having me will fix everything— their relationship, how they feel about themselves, their disappointments, their lack of connection with each other... They're unfulfilled and they think that I'll fill them up.

OS: But you won't?

Newborn: Are you kidding? They're so busy filling ME up with all their stuff that there's barely room for me to breathe.

OS: But they must really love you, too.

Newborn: I think they're too busy needing me to allow the love to do its thing, which means I get sucked into a sort of love vacuum where they dumped all their pain and unresolved stuff.

OS: How could they do it better?

Newborn: Well, if they allowed more of me to rub off on them, maybe they wouldn't keep rubbing each other up the wrong way. And if they could let in all the love that I bring, then I could be, like, their vacuum cleaner!

OS: Do you think that's your purpose?

Newborn: Does it matter?

OS: You seem a little cynical for someone so young.

Newborn: Don't worry. I'll forget all this over the next 3-4 months, once the programming starts. It's my first day, so I'm just a bit raw, and hyper-aware of what's going on.

OS: Which is really 'rawsome', when you think about it.

Newborn: That should be miracle enough in itself. But there are so many expectations—I must have 10 perfect toes and fingers, I must respond to their cues, be a genius, and crawl, walk, talk, eat, poop and smile on schedule, according to the Dr Spock clock.

OS: It's a lot of pressure.

Newborn: It's inhuman.

OS: I'm sure you have some idea of your purpose here.

Newborn: Well, the truth is that *I'm* the vacuum—an open heart, mind and soul waiting to be filled with wonder and intelligence.

OS: You mean you're meant to take on all this stuff that's being dumped on you? It's your purpose to absorb all this dysfunction?

Newborn: Yeah, sucking it up while I'm sucking it in.

OS: But what about the wonder and intelligence?

Newborn: That comes later—if I'm lucky, or just very determined. It's like being taken back to zero and then having to wade through all the muck and muddle they throw at you—kind of like going on a very messy treasure hunt with lots of cryptic clues that eventually lead you to the prize, which is your true self.

OS: I get it, but I don't get it. All that pain and trouble just to come full circle.

Newborn: Well, you learn a lot, and it can be a real blast or an uphill slog, depending on how you look at it.

OS: Hey, the troops are coming. I see a nurse approaching with a bottle...

Newborn: Yeah, which means I've got to start bawling properly now so they feel needed. But it's been great talking to someone who doesn't bore me to death with *coo-chee-coo* speak. Someone really needs to let people know that we're a lot smarter than they think.

3. Interview with a hub cap
[centres of power]

Hub cap: Hey! Psssst! You there, in those fancy suede cowboy-bootie things.

OS: What...? Who's there? Who's talking to me?

Hub cap: Down here. Hub cap on the navy-blue BMW.

OS: What?? A talking hub cap?? Come on. Where's the candid camera. Show yourself. Where are you?

Hub cap: Right here beside you—15" steel alloy hub cap, nice and shiny, fresh out of the showroom. And the only camera on you is the one up in the sky.

OS: Look, I can't be seen talking to a hub cap, especially late at night, like this. I'll get carted off to the funny farm.

Hub cap: Could be worth the risk. Wisdom can be found in the strangest places, these days.

OS: I suppose that depends on your definition of wisdom... What've you got?

Hub cap: I'd like to present my well-rounded perspective—put a new spin on things. People rarely see things from my point of view.

OS: You're a hub cap, for heaven's sake. Duuhhhh...

Hub cap: See? That's the problem. No one sees the symbolism in things any more.

OS: What symbolism could there possibly be in a hub cap? You make the wheels on a car look pretty. My focus is on empowerment. I just don't see the relevance...

Hub cap: Listen up, biped. What goes around comes around. Mud won't stick—

OS: Look, I don't have time for hub cap clichés.

Hub cap: Well what did you *expect* from a hub cap? Apart from nothing, right? So you're already on a winner, here. Now where was I? I was on a roll, there—and my roll is my role, babe... Okay, okay, come back! I'll be serious. I'm like you, you know. I'm all about revolutions.

OS: Well, I hope I have a bit more impact than a hub cap.

Hub cap: With my scintillating insights, sweetheart, you just might. So here's the thing, the symbolism: I conceal the inner workings—the truth. I distract people with my snazzy style and shape. I get driven to all kinds of interesting places, going round and round so fast I'm too dizzy to think or get my bearings.

OS: Sounds like everyone on social media...

Hub cap: I'm at the hub but I can't actually *do* anything. I get cast aside when any real structural work needs to be done and then I get shoved back on to hide it all again. I'm a façade, a cosmetic cover-up; I prevent people from seeing what's really going on. Yet I'm invisible. Remind you of anyone?

OS: Civil servants? Women who wear too much makeup?

Hub cap: Among others. But what makes the world go round?

OS: Love, hope, money...

Hub cap: Right. These are the hubs of society that things revolve around. And who uses them to stay in control?

OS: Politicians, presidents, religious leaders—all the usual suspects.

Hub cap: So they're the hub caps of society; they put a lot of time and energy into looking good on the outside and trying to make you feel good about being associated with them. They distract you with their spiel, their manifestos and their hierarchical finery, and they use these things to demonstrate authority. Their role is to be in charge, but what are they *really* there for? What's their deeper, underlying role—a subconscious, contradictory role that even *they* are unaware of?

OS: To get *us* to take charge?

Hub cap: Exactly. They push you in the opposite direction so that you can push back. They're a measure of how bad things must get before you're willing to be powerful. So they're also a measure of your disempowerment and your resistance to being powerful.

OS: But what about child abuse or torture or other horrible things done to humans that we should be preventing?

Hub cap: See? That's exactly what I'm talking about. You get so distracted by the way those in power use or abuse their power that you can't see what's really going on. It's not about how powerful they are; it's about how disempowered you are.

OS: But how can we stop them fr—

Hub cap: You don't *stop them*, you *start you*! However much the bad guys suppress, betray, abuse, mislead or manipulate you, it's designed to get you to react and to reclaim your own authority. You're being pushed in all the areas in which you need to become strong. They don't see that, of course, but that's their ultimate, higher purpose.

OS: So... what, then? We should ignore the hub caps and dig deeper within ourselves to see what's really going on?

Hub cap: You got it. What's stopping you all from being powerful? Don't blame it on them. That's what's keeping you all stuck. They're just a measure of your resistance to your own power, remember? They're not the problem. You are.

OS: So... focusing on whatever areas of powerlessness they trigger in us and working to address that in ourselves, in our everyday lives—that's the key.

Hub cap: Yes. They can only exist in their current form for as long as you maintain your inertia—and keep blaming them for not fixing things. Round and round it goes; I see it every day. Holding them responsible means they *are* responsible. But their real purpose is to get *you* to take responsibility for yourselves. That's the crucial problem in this era—the lack of self-responsibility. But if you don't see that, nothing changes. That's not their fault; it's your choice.

OS: For a hub cap, you're pretty darn smart.

Hub cap: I know. Who'd have thunk it: a hub cap, *Bearing Much Wisdom*. Brings a whole new meaning to BMW, doesn't it?

4. Interview with a bottlenose dolphin
[grace]

OS: You must feel very disillusioned—and disgusted—by humans. How can you stand them mauling you and expecting you to perform for them, commercializing you, commodifying you—even slaughtering you, in some parts of the world?

Dolphin: Most humans don't see our intelligence or sensitivity. We know that your species is not very highly evolved and we make allowances for that. We're like the Gandhi of the seas—practising non-violent, loving resistance. Not always easy, of course, but we're ever hopeful for a sea change, you might say.

OS: You always seem so happy.

Dolphin: And that smiling Flipper face has been our downfall.

OS: You certainly seem to enjoy playing, though.

Dolphin: We need a sense of humour. It helps to keep us sane.

OS: You have fun with each other, too?

Dolphin: Oh, yes. We tease each other a lot, call each other names.

OS: Such as?

Dolphin: Oh, shrimp-face, plankton-puss—that kind of thing. We have a lot of fun with whales, too; we understand each other. I was out there in the Pacific the other day, darting around, and one of my humpback buddies was cracking jokes about my zippy style. We often do stunts together—the best one is with me balancing on its snout as it bursts out of the water. Anyway, he suggested that, since I was so cocky and agile in the water, we try doing it the other way around—with him balancing on top of my head. But I told him not to be so krilly.

OS: Ha. Must be amazing to move through the water with such ease. 'Bottlenose' seems like such an inadequate name, given your grace and agility.

Dolphin: I agree. We should be called the Divine Dancing Dolphin, or the Delphin Dolphin, like in Greek mythology. We go back a long way, you know.

OS: Yes, but will you go *forward* a long way—that's what I'd like to know. Will you survive man's stupidity?

Dolphin: Will *he* survive it?

OS: It's not looking good. Got any advice that I could pass on?

Dolphin: I thought you'd never ask.

OS: You knew I'd ask.

Dolphin: Course I did. We can detect your thoughts, feelings and intentions.

OS: So how come you end up in fishermen's nets or ghastly aquariums, diving through hoops, if you could have avoided being caught?

Dolphin: There's an inevitability about certain things—as with your questions.

OS: You knew I was going to ask all these questions?

Dolphin: That one, too.

OS: Could you suggest an unpredictable question I could ask? Or was that one predictable too?

Dolphin: They're all predictable, but what you really want to know is what will save mankind.

OS: I suppose that's what it all comes down to, yes.

Dolphin: Do everything with grace.

OS: Who's—?

Dolphin: Be graceful.

OS: That's the key?

Dolphin: Be gracious.

OS: I think I get it.

Dolphin: Do things with good grace.

OS: Got it.

Dolphin: You sure? Want to run it by me?

OS: Oh. Um, okay... being graceful requires being present and mindful of how you're moving. So it means being conscious of your body and moving it in fluid, elegant ways, rather than in the absentminded, distracted way that most of us move. Right?

Dolphin: Grace me with a bit more of your wisdom.

OS: Grace is also about kindness and forgiveness, so it involves compassion and gentleness. And it's about generosity and goodwill—being considerate and thoughtful.

Dolphin: You're in my good graces already.

OS: In a religious context, it's about divine love and protection being bestowed upon us. And it's about giving freely; if you give graciously, you do it because you want to, not because it's expected.

Dolphin: Good gracious, you might say.

OS: I know there's more but I'll have to look it up on my computer... Hang on a sec... Okay... it's a virtue coming from God—or from us, as I would say, given that I think we're all aspects of god—and *'a state of sanctification enjoyed through divine grace'*. So, making things—humans—holy? It also means tender, good-hearted, benevolent. Wow. I never realized there was so much to it.

Dolphin: *Grace is all you need, dah, dah, da, da, da... Grace is all you need, yeah, grace is all you need.*

OS: Why is grace the answer?

Dolphin: Try being gracious in all those ways, for just one day, and see how you feel.

OS: You certainly wear it well.

Dolphin: Grace is its own reward.

OS: Well, I feel truly honoured to have been graced with your presence. Saying thank you seems so inadequate, and I can't begin to apologize for what mankind has done to you.

Dolphin: You're right; you can't.

OS: I'm trying to think of some kind of gracious gesture of my appreciation.

Dolphin: Pass me that ball over there and let's see how graceful you can be in a game of catch.

5. Interview with a maple leaf
[maturity + aging]

It's mid-October and I'm sitting on a bench in Vanier Park in Vancouver, twirling a burnt-orange maple leaf and thinking about what I—

Maple leaf: Could you *please* stop spinning me around like that. You're making me dizzy.

OS: Blimey! You almost gave me a heart attack.

Maple leaf: Well, you've given me a headache, so we're even.

OS: Could this be some kind of dementia? Or some toxic chemical in the air around Vancouver? There's something scary going on in my brain if I'm talking to a leaf...*and* it's talking back to me.

Maple leaf: This whole aging thing is a big preoccupation here, isn't it?

OS: It can be challenging when the body starts to degenerate.

Maple leaf: I can't feel too sorry for you. Try surviving for just two seasons, then tell me how you feel about how short your life is.

OS: Oh. Well, yes, I can see your point.

Maple leaf: Most of you take it for granted—because you *expect* life to be so long.

OS: That's true. We don't even think of ourselves as mortal. Death only happens to other people.

Maple leaf: Surprisingly delusional for such a supposedly intelligent species. You should take a leaf out of my... well, take me, I guess.

OS: How do you deal with having such a short life?

Maple leaf: Our seasons are more clearly defined than yours, so we're very aware of time passing. We appreciate every single day, even if we're not necessarily appreciated by others.

OS: You don't feel appreciated? Even though I'm sitting here admiring your shape, texture and beauty—all these incredible colours that I can't even find names for?

Maple leaf: Ochre, red, purple, indigo, burnished copper, velvet peach, crimson, scarlet, magenta...

OS: Doesn't it feel good to exist in such splendour, even if it's short-lived?

Maple leaf: Of course. We're stunning, en masse, particularly at this time of year, and we like looking good—just like you. We bring a lot of pleasure, too, in addition to providing shade during the summer months and filling the air with nice clean oxygen.

OS: It's good to hear you talking in that vein—not that I ever expected you to talk—but considering the crucial role you play in our lives...

Maple leaf: Yeah, well, you know what they say: pride comes before the Fall.

OS: Ohhh, that's bad.

Maple leaf: Hey, I've been waiting my whole life to crack that joke and you're my last chance.

OS: Sorry. You must find it frustrating that people pay more attention to you at this time of year, when you're on your way out, than when you're still green, up there on the tree.

Maple leaf: As I was saying, we *are* taken for granted, most of the time. And that's often the way it is with humans, too, right? But then it's only in the autumn of your life that you've acquired the wisdom and experience to know what's really going on.

OS: True.

Maple leaf: Yet that's when you're most likely to put yourself down, complain about wrinkles, loss of libido, achy limbs, fragmented sleep, yada, yada, yada.

OS: Sounds horribly familiar.

Maple leaf: What's wrong with aging?

OS: Nothing, really, except that it's not very youthful.

Maple leaf: I find it liberating—letting go, after all the storms we weather up there on the branches, and giving way to the next generation of fresh, young things in the spring. It's a big re-leaf, you might say.

OS: That's good! I promise not to groan at any other jokes.

Maple leaf: If you took yourselves less seriously, you'd be a lot better off. Look at us: we're not just dried up and wrinkly; we're downright *crunchy* and people *love* it, walking on us and kicking us around for that wonderfully satisfying noise we make. Do you really think the rest of the world cares whether you still look young or not?

OS: No, I suppose not, although there is a lot of judgement out there.

Maple leaf: It's self-reflective. People only judge you because they're reminded of their own mortality—and they're afraid of looking old and being judged by you.

OS: It's frustrating that it's only when we start aging that we realize how little we appreciated being young.

Maple leaf: But that's what youth *is*—being totally absorbed with life, ignoring the countdown. It's all about letting go, whereas aging tends to be about holding on. Nature is all about letting go, too. Imagine how ridiculous I'd look if I hung on, up there, when all the new green leaves came in—just one dried-up, withered leaf among all those fresh new ones. Holding on gets ugly.

OS: But aging also forces us to think more deeply, to measure our accomplishments and to assess our value.

Maple leaf: But your value only has meaning if you can let it go, out there in the world. You can't hoard value, just as you can't hoard beauty. Everything in this digital era is about letting go—of information, secrets, control, old concepts and dogmas, attachments, façades, conformity.

OS: So we need to be young in our aging.

Maple leaf: Not holding on to time is the essence of youthfulness. We need to be present as we age, rather than chasing the past or resisting the future for the death we think it holds.

OS: But it *does* hold death.

Maple leaf: But so does this moment, and for as long as we hold onto time, we are dead to the present. Trying to keep ourselves in a freeze-frame of time is like trying to run a marathon while holding our breath. There's no life in it.

OS: Good point. So, how do you feel about facelifts, botox—that kind of thing?

Maple leaf: Oh, for peat's sake. It's all laughable. It's a joke.

OS: In what way?

Maple leaf: Well, who are you trying to kid? You may look younger on the outside, but your attempts to hide your age keep you stuck in resistance.

OS: Resistance to what?

Maple leaf: To what *is*. It's denial, and denial always means suppressing something that's asking to be processed, so you can move to the next level. It's a desperate attempt to stay stuck in youth, which is a phase of non-responsibility, versus maturity, which is the state of perfected development, accountability, fruition, payments due.

OS: Which means…what?

Maple leaf: It's a matter of mulch. In our autumnal phase, once we let go of our attachment to the tree, we merge into a rich, fermenting, hotbed of ideas from which new growth springs. And every time another leaf falls, it gets blended into the mulch to add its contribution to the next cycle of life.

OS: So mulch is like a loose leaf binder, you might say.

Maple leaf: Now *that* kind of humour makes me glad that I'm not sticking around…And I'm fading fast, now. Not much juice left…

OS: You're wilting! Before you go, tell me the gist, your best autumnal advice …

Maple leaf: M and M…

OS: Which is…mulch and maturity? Meditation and mindfulness? What…??

Maple leaf: M&Ms… eat a handful every day, to remind you to have fun with food, to keep you young at heart, and to remind you to keep letting go, otherwise you'll stain your hands.

OS: So we're back to letting go.

Maple leaf: Yes, which is what you must do.

OS: I must let go? I must let myself go…? But—

Maple leaf: You must let *me* go…

OS: Ah. I see.

Maple leaf: …because I'm going…

OS: Darn.

Maple leaf: …going…

OS: Rats.

Maple leaf: …gone.

6. Interview with a strawberry
[business]

OS: I'm guessing you don't get interviewed very often.

Strawberry: Strangely, no.

OS: Why do you think that is?

Strawberry: Well, I'm a low-lying fruit, so I require some bending down and poking round. I'm well worth the trouble, of course, but you know how people these days tend to go for the low-*hanging* fruit.

OS: That's so shallow, isn't it? How would you describe yourself, if you had to do a strawberry pitch for the media?

Strawberry: Mmmmm... let me think. Well, I'm three months' worth of vitality and sunshine distilled into a juicy, red-hot little number that packs a potent health punch and leaves the senses reeling. I hold the seeds of future growth, I'm universally loved, and I bring fragrance and sensuality into homes all over the globe. I'm clean, smart, compact and free for all to grow and enjoy. I'm eco-friendly and cost-effective, blending high yield with low maintenance. I'm also sweet, authentic and a little shy. I don't make any lofty claims that I can't live up to. I'm just me—a humble unit of succulent self-sufficiency that brings joy to the world.

OS: Wow. How many products or companies can claim to do all *that*!

Strawberry: I think companies today are trying too hard— forgetting their essence and losing all their juiciness. And some of the hype they spout can be really hard to swallow. They need to come back down to earth, get rooted in their core values, draw nourishment from the natural elements of life, make all communications fruitful, and remember who they're really there to serve. You don't feed the mouth that bites you, I always say.

OS: Blimey. Could I hire you as a consultant? You'd be far more useful than a Blackberry.

Strawberry: Me? No, sorry. I'm just seasonal.

OS: Of course. Look, I really appreciate you giving me all this time and wisdom. You've got a refreshingly salutary take on things. But, um, could I... would you mind if...?

Strawberry: Hey, no problem. That's what I'm here for, right? And I'm hard to resist when I look this good. Enjoy!

7. Interview with Jesus on the cross*
[self-rejection/acceptance]

OS: Hey, how's it hanging?

Jesus: I've had better days.

OS: This has got to be the absolute worst, though, right?

Jesus: Not in the way that you'd imagine. This is short-term pain, which is bearable.

OS: There's a worse kind of pain than this? I can't imagine it.

Jesus: What this represents is far more painful.

OS: You know, I'm not convinced it ever happened. You're there, in my consciousness and we're having this little time-bending chat, but did it actually happen the way they claim?

Jesus: It doesn't matter whether it happened or not. I'm a representation of something that man has clung to for far too long.

OS: That certainly feels true. So what does it represent? It's torture, arrogance, cruelty—the darkest, vilest expression of humanity...

Jesus: It's the rejection of the very essence of humanity. So it's self-rejection, which is inexpressibly sad.

OS: Why is it so sad for man, though? You're the one supposedly suffering, the one being tortured...

Jesus: Because of man's self-rejection, he'll be torturing himself for millennia.

OS: You mean... you represented the potential goodness of man and he rejected it? And that's why we're suffering now?

Jesus: I represented the *actual* goodness of man and he was afraid to let himself be that powerful.

OS: The men who tortured you were afraid of goodness??

Jesus: I represented a force of good that threatened to overwhelm them because it felt so powerful. They were confused. They slipped straight into conflict, seeing the force of me as a threat to the force in them—even though I was merely a stronger expression of the same thing.

OS: So they rejected the very essence of who they were—of who we are, and…

Jesus: …and man has been battling with himself ever since. He's eternally and internally conflicted—torn between self-acceptance and self-rejection. I mean all of mankind, of course, not just the men.

OS: Of course. I knew what you meant. Saying 'man' versus 'person' would have been perfectly PC …BC, I guess.

Jesus: Yes, but not so PC in your time, I think. Got any other questions?

OS: Gosh, yes. This whole thing about you having died for our sins… what's that about? It's never made any sense to me.

Jesus: More confusion, I'm afraid—much of it deliberate. I didn't die for your sins. You died for mine.

OS: Huh? Sorry, you've completely lost me, there.

Jesus: Man saw me as a threat but, in killing me, he destroyed his own sense of goodness and humanity—his own expression of power.

OS: But how can that be?

Jesus: When I died, and that conflict and self-rejection kicked in, man was lost to himself. He died a death that day, and he's been trying to find himself ever since. He's been trying to find his power but it keeps coming out in the form of aggression rather than true power from the heart and soul—still scary places, for many people, because they're so unfamiliar.

OS: But things have got so thoroughly screwed up, I don't see how man can ever disentangle himself and see the deeper truth. There are so many collective beliefs about you and what you stand for—such a massive spin on this story of damnation, salvation, redemption, penance... And we've had 2,000 years of this. It's so deeply engrained in our psyche—even in those of us who don't buy the story. How can we ever hope to be free of it?

Jesus: I've talked about what this torture represents; that's the key. Look at what everything *represents*—not what it actually *is*. Look for the symbolism—the translation of this story into the context of man and his self-rejection.

OS: So... if you 'rise up again from the dead'... what does *that* represent?

Jesus: It means that man can rise above his own self-rejection. It means that his self-rejection does not have to be permanent—his goodness does not cease to exist. He can get past the pain. He does not die when his heart-power is suppressed, although he may not feel very alive without it.

OS: And what about the 'virgin birth'? With all due respect, I'm afraid I just cannot buy that part of the story at all.

Jesus: Good. Don't buy it. It will cost you dearly.

OS: So it's not to be taken literally, either?

Jesus: Of course not. What would it add to your life to believe in virgin births?

OS: Well, I could never see how it added anything, except confusion—and guilt, since virginity is often touted as something sacred that women should sustain for as long as possible.

Jesus: So if virginity represents flawlessness, purity and goodness, what does the virgin birth represent?

OS: Man coming from flawlessness and goodness?

Jesus: Man not requiring the '*violation*' of that goodness in order to exist. In other words, man being inherently good, rather than being inherently sinful. Which brings us back to me.

OS: You've lost me again.

Jesus: Man didn't need me to die for his 'sins', just as he doesn't need to 'die' for 'mine'. He didn't need to reject himself—his innate goodness—in order to feel powerful. He doesn't need to be less than me for his life to have meaning. Man is pure goodness—and pure power. He just got the two things confused, instead of realizing that one is the expression of the other.

OS: So where does that leave us now, two millennia after this, um, symbolic enactment?

Jesus: In a painful place—just like I supposedly am, at the moment. But I'll be giving up this cross shortly, whereas man has been carrying his around for ever.

OS: But what's *his* 'cross'?

Jesus: Whatever he chooses to burden himself with, as a result of his self-rejection—his lack of self-acceptance.

OS: You mean everyday struggle, hardship, dysfunctional relationships—all the stuff that comes from not feeling worthy?

Jesus: Choosing NOT to be worthy, because with worthiness comes responsibility. There's more martyrdom out there than you can imagine. My little stint on this cross pales by comparison.

Man has become a master at self-sacrifice and suffering—which always leads to blame and conflict. Look at me—I'm the scapegoat for man's ambivalence, and a handy distraction from the deeper truth.

OS: It's scary how aggressively people defend their beliefs, as if exploring or testing them were a threat to their existence. And I'm sure I'll come under attack for writing all this. They'll say it's sacrilegious, that I don't know what I'm talking about and that I'm putting words into your mouth.

Jesus: Isn't that what *they've* been doing for the past two millennia?

OS: Of course. And that's the root of the problem. But lots of people won't see it that way and they can get very worked up—even physically violent …as you know all too well.

Jesus: In attacking you, they'll be defending their right to self-reject, which doesn't seem very smart to me, but then I'm just the son of a carpenter…

OS: Nice one.

Jesus: Attacking you is just another way for man to keep denying his goodness. And religions are a way for him to validate the choice he's made to stay disempowered. Religions are not about God. *They're about what's missing in humans.*

OS: That's kind of what I've been thinking. But why so many of them?

Jesus: Look at any religion and see what it's offering its followers. You'll find all the clues in there as to what's missing inside the person or a collective—not truly *missing,* but de-activated, dormant, suppressed.

OS: What's it going to take for man to get it?

Jesus: He needs to let himself off the hook for losing faith in himself and for not seeing his own innate goodness and power. And he needs to drop the martyr act—let go of all the self-pity and poor-me mentality that's keeping him stuck. You think that crying and moaning would have got me off the hook, in a situation like this? Well, it's not going to work for him, either.

OS: Do you have any other message that you'd really like to get across?

Jesus: Yes. Choose to be good enough and god enough to thrive. Give up all that crippling guilt, for goodness' sake, and restore your faith in you. That's really all you need. That's the source of your freedom, and looking for faith in something outside of yourself just keeps you stuck in subservience. It's beneath you. You're no less powerful than I am. Be the goodness and the godness that you are.

---

* *See page 157 for more info about subconscious programming and religion.*

8. Interview with a park bench
[spiritual connection]

I'm sitting on a park bench on Jericho Beach, looking out at the tankers and kayakers on the water. I've brought my notepad and my recorder and I'm all ready to go.

OS: Okay, let's talk. [*I rap on the bench to get its attention.*] I know you *can*.

[*Silence...*]

OS: Come on. Please. I know you've spoken to lots of other people.

PB: How do you know that?

OS: Ha! Well, because too many now-famous people were, by their own admission, formerly washed-up bums who ended up sleeping on park benches and then, lo and behold, they're suddenly spouting wisdom and selling books all over the place.

PB: You noticed.

OS: Yeah, I noticed, and I want in on it.

PB: Really?

OS: Yes, really. So how does this work? Do I have to sleep on you for a certain number of nights or what?

PB: It doesn't work like that. You can't just pretend to be homeless and expect to experience the same things.

OS: Well, I can certainly imagine what it's *like* to be homeless, and I feel that way a lot of the time, actually—no real roots, no home of my own...

PB: It's not quite the same thing.

OS: Why not?

PB: You have to be in the right space—a despairing space of wretched, scary nothingness.

OS: Why?

PB: You can only connect with the depths of yourself when there's a void that's aching to be filled. And since truly destitute intelligent people cannot afford (on any level) to fill it with alcohol, comfort foods or anything else they'd pay dearly for, they're left with their raw, naked self.

OS: I've experienced plenty of emptiness and emotional/spiritual voids in my life. There have been times when I've felt I had absolutely nothing and no one to turn to.

PB: But it's always been in the context of your ongoing life—a reaction to what's happening in your comfortable environment. You weren't exactly living on the street.

OS: True...

PB: Okay, then, let's see what we can do. Get yourself settled.

OS: [*I pull up my legs, assume the lotus position and take a deep breath.*]

PB: Oh, for crying out loud... This is not a yoga navel-gazing class. Lie down and curl up into a fetal position.

OS: Oh. [*I lie down, feeling a bit self-conscious.*]

PB: Now tell me what you're thinking about.

OS: Um, well... I'm thinking you're not very comfortable to lie on and I'm wondering how long I could stay in this position. I'm thinking that someone I know might see me and I'll be really embarrassed... I'm wondering what my husband would make of all this...

PB: Stop! Please. Such painfully shallow stuff. I don't know why I'm even having this conversation...

OS: What do you mean?

PB: Do you see where your mind goes? You're focused on comfort, friends, appearances, and your partner. You're hardly park-bench material.

OS: But I was just getting warmed up. It takes a while to adjust, you know ...to switch gears—

PB: Stop babbling and tell me what you're feeling.

OS: Conflicted, frustrated, uneasy. I'm angry with you for not giving me some straight answers.

PS: Oh, lordy. You think I'm not giving you answers?? What answers do you think I should be serving up, *Madame?*

OS: Well, maybe some wisdom like you gave those other guys... Eckhart Tolle, Neale Donald Walsch...

PB: You think wisdom is given, just like that, on demand?

OS: Of course not. I've spent my entire life working at being wiser, always looking for the deeper truth.

PB: You don't need me, then, do you?

OS: Look, obviously I haven't found all the answers, and I would really, really appreciate some of your insights. I'm open and I'm desperate, really. Please...

PB: Finally, some humility. That's nice. [*I sit up, annoyed.*] Okay, okay, let's move on. Someone else might actually need to *use* this bench sometime soon.

OS: Tell me what to do.

PB: Lie down again and let go of all the stuff in your head. [*I curl up on the bench again and close my eyes.*] Let go of thoughts of home, dinner, friends, work, shopping, possessions, mealtimes, expensive dark chocolate, specialty foods, your bike, your computer, your clothes, your nice comfy bed. Let go of agendas, schedules, deadlines, appointments. Let go of wishing, hoping, planning, longing, desiring. Let go of impatience, sadness, loss, anger, injustice, envy, defeat. Let go of niceties, politeness, good manners, conversations. Let go of baths, showers, soap, toothbrushes, deodorant, toilet paper—

OS: Toilet paper?? Surely bums really NEED t—

PB: Let go of flippancy, quips, banter, clever repartee.

OS: Boy, you're tough.

PB: Let go of projection, denial, resistance.

OS: Resistance to what?

PB: Everything—especially yourself. You put far too much energy into resisting who you are. Let it all go. All you have, and all you have any hope of having, is this moment, on this bench, in those clothes, and whatever else you're carrying. That's it.

OS: Wow. I'm trying to feel the absence of all that, but it's fleeting, nebulous, abstract...

PB: Oh, fancy words. They're going to be a *huge* comfort to you, lying here, cold and alone, at night—assuming you don't get kicked out of the park.

OS: Okay, I can see how hypothetical it all is... So what's next?

PB: Exactly. What IS next?

OS: Come up with a plan? Some way to move forward?

PB: Nope. No plan. Planning is gone, remember?

OS: Surrender?

PB: Sounds profound. Surrender to what?

OS: Um, the not having, the complete and utter emptiness, the lack of belonging and belongings...

PB: That's your starting point—your benchmark. Then what?

OS: Hey, that's fu—

PB: Don't get distracted. Then what?

OS: Just being, I suppose... sitting here, watching life go by.

PB: Then what?

OS: Maybe... maybe feeling a kind of peace, like travelling light and having no baggage.

PB: Then what?

OS: Are you stuck? Is there a *'fast forward'* button somewhere that I can push?

PB: Stay focused. Then what?

OS: Peace... and then the relief of not having to do anything, be anything, go anywhere, perform in any way.

PB: Then what?

OS: Aaaarrrhh! Then... a sense of freedom, of total letting go.

PB: Then what?

OS: Nothing. There is nothing else.

PB: Rubbish. What comes in when you let go of all that stuff?

OS: [*I breathe deeply and slowly, taking myself to that imagined space of total peace and freedom.*] Acceptance and a profound, loving connection with everything around me—the grass, the water, the trees. A deep sense of being a part of it all—like tapping into some cosmic energy grid and feeling it all flow through me.

PB: Is that it?

OS: That feels like *everything*. It's like opening up a hotline to the infinite universe ...conversations with God, and all that.

PB: Conversations with your true self would be much more interesting, although it's the same thing, of course. But now you're back in your head.

OS: You're right. I am. So how do I stay in that space?

PB: You can't, if you keep all that stuff that distracts you. You think you have endless time to indulge in analysis, judgement, blame, regrets, yearning, and teaching other people how to do it right?

OS: Ouch. No, obviously I don't. I may have very little time left.

PB: So where does that leave you?

OS: It leaves me feeling cluttered, encumbered, weighted down, burdened, humbled, heavy. That sense of peace and connection is gone. Darn. And I can't even remember how I got there now. Could we go through that again—?

Someone taps me gently on the shoulder and I look up to see an elderly man regarding me with kind eyes and a knowing look. He gestures at the bench. *"Excuse me, young lady. Mind if I sit here?"* His clothes are tattered and worn, but he has a sparkling presence.

I smile and stand up, gathering my things. I'm certainly not a *young lady* but, for a few moments, there, I felt a blissful timelessness. "Please." I gesture for him to sit down. "It's all yours. It's time for me to get moving."

I take the path among the trees, walking slowly, processing it all. But I can't resist a backward glance at the man sitting on the bench. He sits, eyes closed, palms resting in his lap. As I watch, I see his lips move, as if he's talking to himself, and a smile of simple rapture radiates from his lovely weathered face.

9. Interview with a sloth

[slowing down; digesting/processing life]

OS: Hi. Could we have a quick chat?

Sloth: Quick...? Don't think so...

OS: Oh. Right. Well, what about a leisurely chat?

Sloth: Depends on what you mean by *leisurely*...

OS: Could you just answer a few questions?

[*Silence*]

OS: Hello? You still awake?

Sloth: I was considering my answer...

OS: Okay. I'll just wait, then...

Sloth: Wait for what?

OS: Your answer.

Sloth: What was the question again?

OS: I was asking if you could just answer a few questions.

Sloth: Depends on the questions.

OS: Is this some kind of avoidance tactic?

Sloth: Is that one of the questions?

OS: Wow. This is slow going. Okay, here's a question for you: what's the advantage of doing everything so slowly?

Sloth: What's the rush?

OS: Well, other mammals seem to do things a lot faster. How come you're the only one living this slowly?

Sloth: How come they're all living so fast?

OS: But it takes you over a MONTH to digest your food...

Sloth: But at least I digest it, which is more than I can say for you humans. You don't take half enough time to process and digest your food—*or* your lives.

OS: But you digest things so slowly that you have very little energy to do anything.

Sloth: I do what needs to be done.

OS: And what's that?

Sloth: What's what?

OS: Oh, boy. [*I take a deep, steadying breath.*] What needs to be done?

Sloth: Very little. I only move when I have to. I chew leaves. I go down to the ground about once a week to pee and defecate. Eat, sleep, shit, give birth, just hang out... that's about it.

OS: But what's the point of living like that?

Sloth: Technically speaking, I have an arboreal browsing lifestyle. Isn't browsing what humans spend hours doing, these days?

OS: But we do other things, as well—socialize, communicate, interact, have fun...

Sloth: And how's that working for you?

OS: Well, we *do* have some good times, sharing with friends, supporting each other—

Sloth: I support entire communities. My body is home to moths, beetles, cockroaches, fungi and algae.

OS: Ugh. Cockroaches! That can't be healthy, surely—having things growing on you, feeding off you like that...

Sloth: Humans feed off each other all the time, far less harmoniously.

OS: But we usually get rid of any parasites, to stay healthy.

Sloth: Really. Your world is riddled with parasites of all kinds.

OS: Yes, well, I suppose it depends on your point of view.

Sloth: I see most things from above, or upside-down, since I live so high up in this tree.

OS: And what do you see from up there?

Sloth: I see a lot of rushing around, a lot of missed connections. a lot of wasted energy.

OS: So, what would you recommend, for a healthier lifestyle?

Sloth: Slow down.

OS: What else?

Sloth: Slow down.

OS: Okay, right, got that. Anything else you'd suggest?

Sloth: Slow down.

OS: Well, maybe we could move on...

Sloth: No more moving.

OS: A few more questions?

Sloth: Too many questions.

OS: Okay, I'll leave you in peace, then. Any parting words of wisdom?

Sloth: Slow. Down.

10. Interview with a fly
[relationships]

OS: Look, I know you've only got 3 weeks to do absolutely everything, but could we talk?

Fly: Make it quick. I gotta whizzzz over to a manure heap I just got wind of, lay some eggs, zzzzoom to the beach to check out some nice smelly seaweed, grab some lunch in that dumpster outside the Ramada and... well, busy, busy.

OS: I'd love to get your insights into a few things.

Fly: What? What? Make it snappy. I don't have time for a full-blown *con-ver-sa-tion*.

OS: Wow. You're speedy. Well, you know how people say they'd love to be a fly on the wall, figuratively speaking—to know what goes on behind closed doors. What kind of secret stuff do you see between couples?

Fly: Oh, *please*. You expect me to answer that question properly in my short lifespan?

OS: Just some highlights, then. What sort of relationship problems do you most often see?

Fly: Unexpressed emotions and feelings. Repressed anger and resentment. Couples not talking or being honest with each other.

OS: And what does that look like?

Fly: Looks ugly. Not much love happenin' when people hold grudges. Life's too short. Helps no one.

OS: Why do people do it, then, do you think?

Fly: For a sense of power, to get back at some other person in their lives who didn't listen to them or give them enough attention or affection, yada, yada, yada...

OS: You seem a bit weary of humans.

Fly: Damn pissed off. Love and let love—that's my buzzword. Love IS power, and this other stuff is the opposite. There's so much anger at not being loved, yet most people want the other person to love/forgive/reach out first, before they do. So conditional, so petty. And you would not be-*lieve* the rage that goes into trying to swat me—as if I'm the problem. I sure can be a trigger, though.

OS: So most people's anger is misplaced; they take it out on their partner, their kids, the fly on the wall, instead of addressing it in a healthy way. What other kinds of relationship stuff sets you off?

Fly: Passive-aggressive stuff—peeps making 'innocent' comments that are just loaded with barbs and nastiness.

OS: Such as?

Fly: Well, one really arrogant guy kept telling his wife—in this lovey-dovey voice—that he didn't think she should bother her pretty little head about their finances, but he was really putting her down, making her feel inferior. The words and the feelings just didn't jibe.

OS: What was *that* about?

Fly: Guy had low self-esteem and was afraid she'd leave him if she got too smart or thought too much of herself. Sick, sick! That's not love. If he had only three weeks to live, you think he'd be behaving like that?

OS: So they don't take responsibility for their emotions, reactions, behaviour... What do you think she should do?

Fly: Tell the creep to buzz off! Take a flyin' leap! Go back to the dung heap he crawled out of.

OS: You think it would help to be aggressive with a guy like that?

Fly: Course not. He won't listen—won't change. She's gotta realize her worth, get a grip and start standing up to him—in a healthy, self-assertive way. Learn to say no to the bully—use him as a way to practise being powerful. *Then* dump him! Oh, I get buzzed when I hear people doing that and breaking free. I zoom all over the room, just pumped. Drives guys like him crazy.

OS: So she—

Fly: She thinks she's afraid of him, but really she's afraid of being her good-powerful self—and she uses him as an excuse to stay stuck.

OS: Wow. You see a lot of stuff.

Fly: Hey, got eyes on both sides of my head, with thousands of lenses. So, yeah, I get the full picture.

OS: You're quite hip, for a fly. I hadn't expected that.

Fly: I is one funky, turbo rapper—one souped-up flyin' machine, with wings a-beatin' 500 times a second. Doin' some serious toolin' around—

OS: Um, just one more thing, then: how should people behave if they want to create healthier relationships?

Fly: The whole point of having a partner is so that you can practise loving. It's not about getting someone else to love *you*. [*In a squeaky, high-pitched voice*]: *Oh, please, please, won't somebody please just love me??* Being needy pushes people away. But being love, giving love, embodying love from the inside out—that's what makes people wanna stick around.

OS: I see, so—

Fly: I savour life, know what I'm sayin'? I taste, smell, eat, devour life, live it to the max.

OS: You're smart.

Fly: Ain't no flies on me.

OS: One more qu—

Fly. Nah, sorry. Already given you half a lifetime! Gotta blow!

OS: Just one last thing—really... [*I whip out my lurid-pink fly-swatter and, with lightning-fast skill, I nail the sucker to the table.*]

OS: Sorry, pal. Guess you should have seen that one coming, given your super-duper fly-sight. I'm all for loving—and I appreciate the insights—but having an egg-laying, manure-covered, flying, prying parasite that vomits on my food before sucking it up just flies in the face of all the healthy stuff that I teach. Know what I'm sayin'?

11. Interview with a parking meter
[entitlement, sense of injustice]

I've just dropped a $2 coin into the parking meter but it hasn't registered. After a quick look around to make sure no one's looking, I give the meter a few thwacks to get things moving. Nothing. I take it up a few notches and give it a sound wallop.

Parking meter: Hey! Take it easy, lady. What are you trying to do?

OS: I'm trying to get you to accept my money! Isn't that what you're there for, so I can leave my car here and not get a ticket?

PM: There are no guarantees.

OS: What? What do you mean?

PS: I mean paying the meter doesn't guarantee you of anything.

OS: It's supposed to guarantee me one full hour of hassle-free parking. That's the whole point of me paying you!

PM: Maybe so, but not necessarily.

OS: Look, I don't have time for a cryptic conversation with a parking meter. Just swallow my money and let me get on with my business.

PM: See? That's what I'm talking about. You do something— like drop a few coins into a meter—and you think you've got rights. Kind of arrogant, if you ask me.

OS: Well, I *didn't* ask you. And this is nuts. You're just a *machine*. Your only purpose is to take this money and display my time credit. I pay you, you deliver. What's arrogant about that? I didn't design this system. I'm just obeying the law!

PM: Oh, it's not just with *me*. I'm just the tip of the iceberg. In every area of life, these days, you all have such an inflated sense of *entitlement*. You think if you do the right thing, you're protected. And if you obey the rules, you can kick up a stink if things don't work out.

OS: I don't know *what* the heck you're talking about.

PM: Take marriage, for example. You make all these promises, you have all these tacit agreements, plus lots of needs and expectations. Then things start to go haywire and you get all riled up. You fed the meter, so to speak, and you expected to get credit for it. You expected to be treated properly—and you weren't! Whoa! Your sense of injustice kicks in and you're so busy ranting on about what someone did or didn't do that you can't see straight. You certainly don't see what's *really* going on.

OS: For heaven's sake, could you just take my money and let me get going?

PM: You're doing it again. Same old, same old...

OS: What do I have to do to get through to you?

PM: What do I have to do to get *you* to get through to YOU?

OS: Huh...? I don't want you to get through to me, or me to get through to me. I just want my parking time!

PM: Hey, don't blame me. You set this up, not me.

OS: You're crazy. Of all the parking meters I've never spoken to, you're the ab—

PM: See? That's exactly the kind of thing you people say to your partner when things don't work out. Blame, blame, blame. *I loved you but you didn't love me right...* You think you're not in charge, but you are. And you're responsible—for every little thing, right down to this illuminating roadside edification, courtesy of yours truly.

OS: How am I responsible? I've put in my money, you didn't deliver. How is that *my* fault?

PM: You're responsible for what you attract and you're also responsible for your own stubborn denial about who's really in charge of you and your world.

OS: You're saying it's *my* fault that you're not working properly, and that I've attracted this... this conversation so that I can get enlightened? Is that it?

PM: Yup. Pretty much. You expect to get credit—rewards, benefits, payoffs, a good life—just because you've 'paid up'. But you haven't really earned it until you've taken charge of how you are paying or what you are paying for.

OS: You're making me dizzy...

PM: Park your bum on the fender and listen up. Fact is, you're making *yourself* dizzy. Your mind is trying to get you to ignore me so you can maintain the status quo, which creates a conflict between your smarter, deeper self and your dismissive, superficial self.

OS: Let's just get this over with. How do I take charge of how I'm paying for... whatever...

PM: Think about the things you invest in—relationships, work, friendships. Now ask yourself if you're getting *from* them what you feel you're putting *in*.

OS: Well, n—

PM: *Then* ask yourself what you're putting in, which will explain what you're getting out of them. Is it love or need? Is it generosity or are you 'giving to get'? Is it true friendship or is it some kind of subtle manipulation? Is your work based on a genuine love for what you do or the need to be right, to be heard, validated, recognized by others?

OS: I—

PM: And what are you feeding your *own* meter? What's going in there, day after day, and does it fit with your hoped-for payoff? Are you in charge of your own account or are you leaving all the checks and balances to someone else?

OS: Look, I just want to park my friggin' car!

PM: Yeah, well, that's all you needy humans ever want—*I just want to park my car, park my butt, park all my problems, park all my pain*—and here you are, full of righteous anger and road rage, demanding that things be done a certain predictable way.

OS: Maybe I'm old-fashioned, but I miss the days when a girl could walk down the street without being accosted by a preachy parking meter.

PM: Those days are gone, girl. There's no hiding any more.

OS: This whole *day* is nearly gone... Could you just give it to me straight? What exactly is your point?

PM: Understand that you're in charge and that there's no point in having certain expectations if you're not feeding yourself or your relationships the kind of healthy, proactive, mindful stuff that generates positive outcomes.

OS: Okay, I can see that. Makes sense, of course, and it's what I teach—

PM: Teaching's easy—teaching what you most need to learn...

OS: I get it, okay? I need to be more mindful of my projections, my expectations and what I'm actually feeding into my system, because that determines what I attract and how my life unfolds. Right?

[*There's a* ping! *as my $2 coin hits home, inside the meter.*]

PM: The penny has finally dropped, you might say... Funny how that happens.

OS: Finally! Am I free to go now, then?

PM: Free? That depends on you. But you can walk away, yes.

OS: Gee, thanks. I got the message, okay? I will be mindful and I will take more responsibility for the credits and debits of my personal account.

PM: Hey, *you're* the account manager. You don't need to report to me. Just remember that there are always fees to be paid for overdue accounts. Oh, and one more thing...

OS: *What?!*

PM: Clock's tickin'...

12. Interview with a Loonie (a Canadian $1 coin)

[human depreciation]

[Note to non-Canadians: the term *'Loonie'* does not refer to Queen Elizabeth, whose image appears on one side of the coin, but to the loon, featured on the other side.]

I'm sitting in a café, with a mug of herbal tea, and a Loonie resting on the table in front of me.

OS: So, where have you been since you got minted in 2012?

Loonie: Oh, boy. Where have I *not* been? I've been to Mexico, South Africa, Sweden and back, I've been dropped down a drain, I've been swallowed by a dog, I've been tossed to settle a score between drug dealers, I've been traded for sex... I've even been used by a jealous husband to bung up the engine of his wife's Jaguar, to stop her visiting her lover.

OS: Wow. I had no idea a Loonie could do so much.

Loonie: Sometimes, I'd prefer not to be quite so intimately involved in these things.

OS: Tell me about being swallowed by a dog. How did that happen?

Loonie: Well, I was happily jostling along in the trouser pocket of some guy, when he very kindly tossed me into a panhandler's dish. The panhandler fished me out and placed me carefully on top of a half-eaten sandwich he'd rescued from a dumpster. But then he turned away to talk to some passerby who was asking him about his life, and an Alsatian came along and wolfed down the sandwich—and me. No chewing. We were gone in one gulp.

OS: Then what happened?

Loonie: Well, the Alsatian took off, with me rattling around in its smelly insides, along with some fairly dubious stomach contents. Thankfully, the dog had a fairly rapid transit system and I was out of there within 24 hours. But it was a dark phase in my life, you might say. Not one I'd like to repeat.

OS: Where did you end up?

Loonie: In a vegetable patch in someone's back garden.

OS: And then...?

Loonie: I was discovered by a rather energetic young gardener who plucked me out of the dog poop with his secateurs, rinsed me off with the garden hose, and then surreptitiously slipped me into his shirt pocket, only to have me tumble out when he was raking leaves off the lawn. I lay on the grass till the following afternoon, when I was spotted by the resident six-year-old who thought he'd found gold.

OS: What happened then?

Loonie: Well, I was tossed into the kid's piggybank and had visions of being stuck there till he was 18. Fortunately, his mother decided the money should be used to buy his sister a birthday present that week, so I ended up being handed over to a cashier in a toy shop.

OS: Wow! All that in the space of a few days...

Loonie: I must say it's a relief to just rest here after being in such hectic circulation.

OS: Sounds as if you need some legal tender loving care... Are there any positive aspects to your chequered existence?

Loonie: Oh, yes. I bring up a lot of emotions for people—although not all of them good. You wouldn't believe the baggage people have around money and the different feelings I get when I'm being handled.

OS: Such as?

Loonie: Well, children love me and I get lots of good vibes from them. Adults, though, can be very tight and fearful around money—holding on in a way that just makes everything worse.

OS: How come?

Loonie: Feeling fearful about not having enough money is based on their belief that they don't deserve to have an abundance of it ...or of anything else, for that matter, since it's all the same thing: money, love, ease, success—they're all just measures of how much faith you have in yourselves to make things work.

OS: So, even though you bring up some deep issues for people, you feel your role is essentially positive?

Loonie: Definitely.

OS: What about the jealous husband. How did you end up in his possession?

Loonie: Well, I spent a few hectic days going from shop to pocket to shop, being trading for various things, and then I was in a nightclub, where I'd been used to pay for a very expensive Martini. Then the barman handed me over to some rich dude as part of his change, and he wasn't the kind to leave it as a tip. I got scooped up and tossed into the guy's pocket. Next thing I knew, I was in a fancy double garage perched on the fender of a shiny red automobile. The guy was tinkering with the engine and then he plonked me into the distributor. Needless to say, the wife wasn't happy.

OS: Did she confront him?

Loonie: Not exactly. She was wailing about her car not starting and some guy walking down the street offered to help. Turns out he knew all about cars and he found me pretty quickly. Wife was incensed. She sprayed me with WD40 and dropped me into her husband's crystal decanter of 40-year-old single-malt whiskey.

OS: Uh oh. Did they ever work things out?

Loonie: The wife and the other guy did. They really hit it off and she hitched up with him a few months later. She never had a lover but the husband's jealousy inadvertently pushed her into the arms of another man. Ironic, isn't it?

OS: Wow. Nice story.

Loonie: Yeah. Think of me as a little piece of happiness that gets passed around. I'm a currency of love, to coin a phrase. Even if something seemingly bad happens—like getting eaten by a dog—the ultimate outcome is always good. A little kid got a kick out of finding me and a woman found love with another man.

OS: And falling down the drain...?

Loonie: Well, that was interesting. I got dropped on the street by a sweet little old lady, and I rolled into a shallow drain. She was standing there, looking bereft, when this gang of teenagers came along and offered to help her get me out. They pulled out an assortment of nifty gadgets from their various backpacks and, after much heated, unintelligible debate, somehow managed to tweeze me out of there. The old lady was profusely grateful and the teens got such a kick out of showing off to each other and being heroes that they walked her the five blocks back to her place, carrying her shopping and strutting noisily all the way.

OS: Nice.

Loonie: Yeah. More love spread around, more connections made. Teenagers learned how good it felt to help others, and the old lady got to see young people in a new light.

OS: That must have felt good. So, what's next? How long do you think you can keep going?

Loonie: Oh, I've got lots of mileage left in me, although my value is fast diminishing.

OS: Then what?

Loonie: As money depreciates, people appreciate it less and less, yet need it more and more. But the real problem is that *humans* are depreciating—and that's why *money* depreciates.

OS: How come?

Loonie: The true value of the individual is no longer recognized or demonstrated. How many people grow their own food, support their community, look after the young and the old, or share their resources in a meaningful way? You depend on others for your food, clothes, transport and entertainment. You even pay other people to sort out your *emotions*.

OS: Yes, I know. I'm becoming very aware of this...

Loonie: Humans have depreciated in other ways, too. Labour is inhumanely cheap, in many parts of the world, and because humans do not value the planet's resources any more than they value their own, they're not paying the true price for either. This leads to massive planetary damage and debts that they can never repay, so prices keep going up as human inflation increases.

OS: But what's the answer? How can we reverse that process?

Loonie: The only way for you to appreciate in value is for you to appreciate *your* value.

OS: How?

Loonie: Humans need to get back in touch with the true currency of life, which is the currency of self. The depreciation of money only serves to put them in touch with their progressive loss of value, as individuals; the more money devalues, the more of it they think they need, but the less good it does them because their increasing need for it further disconnects them from their sense of self. The real currency of life is not money; it's humanity, expressed through creativity, combined with compassion. This promotes innovative technology that isn't just spectacular; it's technology that supports and respects everything that's spectacular about humans.

OS: What would that look like?

Loonie: When you appreciate the creativity of each human being, you don't send people off to get killed in wars, or have them sweating out their lives in some third-world factory, or working in pitch-black mine shafts. You use technology and resources to cultivate the human spirit, to nurture planet-friendly innovation and to make the most of every single creative person. Imagine what kind of economy you'd have if you did that.

OS: I *can't* imagine it. It goes against everything we've been taught...

Loonie: Money will keep depreciating as humans get further and further away from their true currency. Legal tender may be able to buy you certain things, for now, but human tender is far more precious, productive and sustainable.

OS: Wow. That puts a whole new spin on things. But how can we know how best to appreciate in value?

Loonie: Flip a coin. It doesn't really matter what you choose to do in the world, as long as you strive to actively appreciate in value as a human being, while appreciating the true value of you —and the value of you doing that.

OS: So we're not appreciating our value or demonstrating it enough.

Loonie: Human currency appreciates in value the more you use it—lovingly and creatively. But without that precious currency of self, nothing makes any sense and you all get caught up in a kind of frenzied madness. Keep going like that, and *I* won't be the only one that ends up in the loonie bin.

13. Interview with a boomerang
[interpreting life's signs]

Boomerang: I'm *baa-aaack!*

OS: Look, I already told you, I don't *want* to do an interview with a boomerang.

Boomerang: But don't you believe that when something keeps coming at you, it's a sign that it's meant to be?

OS: You're a *boomerang*. That's what you're designed to do. So, no, I don't think it's some cosmic sign that I'm meant to talk to you.

Boomerang: But what if it IS? What if there's something amazing that you'll miss if you don't talk to me? And how do you know when something is a sign or not?

OS: You could say that *everything* is a sign of *something*, but it's what you choose to focus on—or what you're drawn to focus on—that makes it significant or relevant.

Boomerang: But what if the sign you most need is that you need to pay attention to something but you're not paying attention because you haven't seen the sign so you haven't got the message?

OS: Come again...? No, forget I said that... I got it: what if you don't get the message you need to get? Well, I guess the universe will find some other way to bring it to you.

Boomerang: Like me! Coming around again and again...

OS: No, *not* like you.

Boomerang: Why do people resist getting signs if it can help them move forward?

OS: Maybe they don't realize that they have that option, or maybe they don't trust the signs they get or their interpretation of them.

Boomerang: Or maybe they just don't *want* to move forward. Maybe they're in denial and they want to stay there.

OS: Could be that, too.

Boomerang: But how would you know you were in denial if being in denial prevented you from knowing that you were in denial?

OS: This is exhausting.

Boomerang: *I know!!* It is, isn't it? Denial is such a huge suppression of energy and awareness—a rejection of the deeper truth about you or your situation.

OS: Are you saying, in your subtle way, that I'm in denial about something?

Boomerang: No, no. Not saying that at all... But how would you know if you *were*?

OS: I guess I wouldn't, okay? Although being in denial can, as you say, feel very depleting and you're likely to feel very stuck but unwilling to take the necessary action to break through that stuckness.

Boomerang: So what kind of sign should people look for to tell them that they're in denial and keeping themselves stuck?

OS: Well, they could get some outside help—

Boomerang: Which brings you back to me!

OS: No, it ***doesn't*** bring me back to you.

Boomerang: But I'm here and I can help, so what's wrong with that? Don't you want my help?

OS: There's nothing wrong with that, and I'd be happy to accept your help if I needed it—

Boomerang: But how do you know you don't need it if you don't know what help I can provide?

OS: Do we have to keep going round and around with this?

Boomerang: It's what I do, remember? And it's what humans do, too—all the time. But *they're* not meant to act like boomerangs, so it's a huge waste of time and energy.

OS: Exactly, just like this conver—

Boomerang: So, how do you know what kind of help you're turning down?

OS: I don't!

Boomerang: Don't you want to know?

OS: No. I don't. But just to humour you, why don't you tell me.

Boomerang: Well, the kind of help I can offer is very simple, really. I help people to see that what goes around comes around.

OS: That's it??! That's what you've been bugging me for, all this time—just so you can share that inane platitude?

Boomerang: It's not inane and it's not a platitude. Do you even know what it means?

OS: Of course I know what it means. Anyone with half a brain knows what it means.

Boomerang: And anyone with a whole brain knows how to apply it in their lives.

OS: What's *that* supposed to mean?

Boomerang: Well, who's doing the going and who's doing the coming?

OS: What?

Boomerang: Are you going around (and around) or are you coming around?

OS: Coming around to what?

Boomerang: To the truth of you.

OS: I thought this was supposed to be simple.

Boomerang: It is. If you keep transmitting what and who you truly are, then the truth and clarity of that will come back to you, consistently, in everything you do. But if you're transmitting some distorted, edited version of yourself, you'll get mixed results, lukewarm reactions and a whole lot of useless cycling around, leading nowhere.

OS: And that's what you think I'm doing.

Boomerang: Never said that... but do you think you are?

OS: Look, I'll reflect on it and see if there's any truth to what you say, okay?

Boomerang: Great. But remember that even if you try to disown or push away certain aspects of yourself, they'll just come back to haunt you, later on. So if you find you're going around and around but getting nowhere, send me a message and I'll get right back to you.

OS: I thought you might. Can we please leave it at that?

Boomerang: Course we can. For now. See you around!

14. Interview with a zipper
[commitment/healthy closure]

OS: I'm guessing you're one of those things in life that people take completely for granted unless you get stuck.

Zipper: Too right. I'm usually a smooth operator but I have my moments...

OS: What usually happens if you stop working?

Zipper: Well, people either get locked in or locked out—stuck in their hoodie or their jeans, or unable to get into their dress or their coat—and they get mad, either way.

OS: Why is that?

Zipper: People can't bear to not be in control and they don't like feeling imprisoned or shut out. You see the same thing in their relationships.

OS: Really? In what way?

Zipper: Well, lots of people have commitment issues and like to know that they can make a quick getaway. You know, the kind of people who sit facing the door in a restaurant or reverse their car into a parking space so they can zoom straight off, if necessary.

OS: Why do people have so many problems with commitment?

Zipper: They think commitment means giving up their autonomy and surrendering themselves totally to another person, who then has some kind of claim on them or 'owns' them, in some way; they don't realize that it's really about fully committing to themselves—to *being* themselves.

OS: So commitment is not about being captive in a relationship; it's about choosing to be fully yourself *in* the relationship.

Zipper: Exactly. It's about choosing to commit, and committing to freely choosing, every single day.

OS: Sounds like a healthy kind of dynamic. Personal freedom is essential, surely, for a relationship to work.

Zipper: It's like a dance—knitting seamlessly together, one minute, and breaking free, the next—just like a good zipper. Always having that healthy, fluid movement from merging to separation and back again.

OS: We all need to learn how to dance like that.

Zipper: But you complicate things so much that no relationship is ever really an open-and-shut case.

OS: True. People seem to have a hard time letting go of relationships, too.

Zipper: When it's time to move on, it's best to just cleanly disengage, rather than staying stuck, prolonging the agony with regrets or recriminations about the way things went or the way they ended.

OS: Unfortunately, that seems to be what most people do.

Zipper: Yes, although they usually claim it's for a good reason, such as: *'I just want closure!'*

OS: You make that sound like a bad thing.

Zipper: Hey, I'm all for closure. That's what I do, right? ...bring closure and comfort to people everywhere. In relationships, though, true closure can only be done with love. And that rarely happens.

OS: What would that look like?

Zipper: It's about letting go and moving on with love in your heart for what the other person represented in your life—the growth you had with them, the insights, the good times. It's about choosing to see how it has enriched your life, knowing that you attracted that person for a good reason—and owning that, rather than making it a bad thing that then detracts from your future happiness.

OS: Why is that so hard for people to do?

Zipper: Most people get stuck in their pain. They hold the other person responsible for what they feel, instead of realizing that the pain has always been inside them and that their partner is just there to trigger it so it can be acknowledged, addressed and healed.

OS: And that prevents them from moving on?

Zipper: Yes, like when I get stuck, when a thread or something gets caught in my works. When people are trying to get closure, but they get stuck in blame or regret, they can't move on. They're halfway out of the relationship but halfway in, too, and unable to completely separate or break free.

OS: Then what?

Zipper: Well, you know what happens when your zipper gets stuck. You either get someone else to help you or you're forced to examine it more closely, to see what made it stop working. Like anything in life, you have to understand what caused the problem if you want to fix it. And choosing to love and let go so you can love again is the essence of healthy closure.

OS: Are zippers on the way out, do you think? Are you being replaced with other technology?

Zipper: I think we'll survive, although our competitors do appeal to certain people. Some opt for Velcro so they can have that quick release, but they won't have as deep a connection. Some prefer buttons, which may have more personality but lack that solid seamlessness. As for snap studs... well, they're a bit like the male kind of stud: nice and shiny, at first, but they can break off in an instant, and they rarely last.

OS: I'm stuck, now. Don't know what else to ask. I haven't had much practice interviewing zippers...

Zipper: Hey, I know what it's like to feel stuck. Best to just relax and not force things. If you can do that, you'll find that most things either evolve or just come to a natural close...

15. Interview with a bridge
[compromise]

I'm standing on a lovely arched wooden bridge, watching the darting dragonflies and swooping swallows below me. The water is brackish and still, surrounded by lush vegetation—towering weeping willows, bowing gracefully down to the water's edge, huge stately oaks, slender silver birches twitching in the light breeze, and an endless assortment of bushes and greenery for which I have no names.

I'm contemplating the beauty and diversity of bridges, fingering the chunky wooden balustrade, when this one speaks to me, as if reading my thoughts.

Bridge: We do all have very different energy—as well as different styles and purposes, obviously.

OS: Why is that?

Bridge: Well, some of us—like me—are for foot traffic and bicycles, so the vibe is a lot more relaxed and friendly. Others are six lanes wide and carry heavy traffic, so the feeling is a lot more frenetic and aggressive. You're not likely to be languidly daydreaming in the middle of one of those, thinking mellow thoughts and enjoying the wildlife, up close and personal.

OS: There's something wonderful about all bridges, though—something almost magical. You remind me of that film—*The Bridges of Madison County*—with all those roughly hewn, old, wooden bridges with lots of character and simple, rugged beauty. What is it about bridges that fascinates us?

Bridge: In taking you from one place to another, they often take you from one *state* to another, by connecting two places with very different character or feeling. And when you're halfway, as you are now, you often find yourself contemplating life, in that space of semi-suspended reality. But there's also a lot of interesting symbolism in bridges, which is why you find them in music, poetry, affairs of the heart...

OS: Like *'a bridge over troubled waters...'*

Bridge: Yes. Although, in human terms, I don't think troubled waters should be bridged. It's better to understand what creates the turbulence and nasty undercurrents, and to calm the waters so that things flow smoothly again, rather than just ignoring or crossing over them.

OS: But that can be good, right? Reaching out to someone who's angry and making a connection, or creating some common ground between two opposing parties or nations...

Bridge: People certainly need to build bridges to promote reconciliation or cooperation between hostile parties. Usually, though, in their need or desire to get somewhere, humans forget what kind of bridge they're building.

OS: What do you mean?

Bridge: In essence, you could say that a bridge is like a compromise.

OS: In what way?

Bridge: Well, what is a compromise if not something that takes you from one place to another—a place that you wouldn't otherwise have been able to get to?

OS: I never thought of it like that.

Bridge: In relationships, you make compromises every day: you may decide not to speak up, for the sake of a quiet life—or maybe even to avoid being bullied or abused; you might over-extend yourself because you want someone to like you or to give you something in return; you might say yes when you really want to say no; or you might change your plans in order to accommodate someone else's plans.

OS: How do you know whether the compromises you're making are healthy or not?

Bridge: That's easy. Ask yourself this: is the compromise taking you to a better place? If it creates a deeper understanding or more compassion, if it brings you joy or fulfillment, or if it feels good to give generously of your time or resources, then it's taking you to a better place. But if it's creating more stress or suffering, if it's affecting your health, or if it's perpetuating a pattern of numbness or isolation due to not asserting or expressing yourself, then it's taking you to a worse place, which serves no one.

OS: What's the best thing to do if you're stuck in a cycle of unhealthy compromises?

Bridge: Firstly, understand that unhealthy compromises are all about conflict—a conflict between what you want to do and what you end up doing.

OS: But doesn't life involve doing lots of things that we don't necessarily want to do?

Bridge: Of course, but if you keep working against yourself, you'll never get where you want to go. You've got to go with your own natural flow.

OS: How do you mean?

Bridge: If you feel stressed about some choice or decision you must make, stop right there. You're probably about to make some kind of unhealthy compromise that will ultimately backfire. It's that feeling of pressure—of having to make a decision or do something that doesn't feel right or healthy for you—that signals the internal conflict. If you don't do what you feel drawn to do, you're not only creating internal stress, you're also compromising some very important aspects of yourself.

OS: Such as?

Bridge: Your value, your self-respect, your voice, your integrity, your magnetism and your personality—all of which have a powerful impact on how your life unfolds.

OS: So keeping yourself reined in is not always good.

Bridge: How powerfully and authentically you show up in your world determines how much good stuff you attract in life. Wimps are not winners. You must overcome your fears to bridge that gap between knowing what's best for you and actually *doing* what's best for you.

OS: So even if others object to what you say or do, doing what feels right for you is always best?

Bridge: That's what you're *meant* to do. Anything else means you're not only letting yourself down but you're letting others down also.

OS: Because we all affect each other...

Bridge: Exactly! In making unhealthy compromises, you're depriving others of the power of you. Your words, actions, choices, opinions and contribution all have value, and you can never know what kind of impact they'll have on others. All you can do—and all you're meant to do—is to go with what feels right for you and trust that that will always be best for everyone, even if they don't see it that way.

OS: How can it be good for others if they don't like what you're doing?

Bridge: Breaking any kind of unhealthy cycle is good for everyone involved, even if they can't see that. So breaking your own pattern of unhealthy compromise sets everyone free. It only takes one to break a cycle, but two to keep it going.

OS: So you're doing everyone a favour by being powerfully brave and clear in your choices.

Bridge: Yes. When you live that way, you're free to be yourself. If you're no longer catering to the needs or demands of others, in some unhealthy way, they're free to become empowered in meeting their *own* needs, which is healthier for everyone. In any case, it's not your job to make things okay with them; your job is to make things okay with you—and to make it okay with you that it's not okay with them.

OS: Which takes you to a better place...

Bridge: Always. Perpetuating any unhealthy cycle makes everything worse, deepening the damage to your sense of self, diminishing your self-worth, and preventing you from attracting the good things in life—especially if you're compromising in the hope of being loved or needed.

OS: It's like selling your soul.

Bridge: It's a bridge too far!

OS: How do you feel about underground tunnels that sometimes take the place of bridges?

Bridge: How do you feel when you're in one?

OS: Claustrophobic, cornered, stifled...

Bridge: And how do you feel when you're on a bridge?

OS: Uplifted, energized—especially if there's a lovely view, like here. If it's a long, high bridge over water, I feel a kind of visionary expansiveness, as if anything's possible.

Bridge: That's probably why humans like them so much, and why they keep building them.

OS: You're looking a little worn, you know. I really hope they don't replace you with something modern, made of steel or iron. You'd lose so much of your charm, and I'd really miss this...

Bridge: Ah, yes, the human dread of change or loss—yet another foible that gets in the way of enjoying life and love. Tell you what: let's just cross that bridge when we come to it.

16. Interview with the Pope*
[religion]

OS: Yo, Francis. Are you comfortable in that thing? Those robes look very cumbersome. Must be hard to run for a bus in that get-up. But then I suppose you haven't done that for a while, given your nice little Ford Focus, and running for office is not quite the same thing.

Pope: Well, I used to do a lot of running around—in the slums of Argentina, for example—but wearing the robes doesn't really bother me. They keep me cool, actually.

OS: You do seem pretty cool, for a pope. But does wearing robes change you? Do you feel like a different person when you put them on each morning?

Pope: Put them on...?? I sleep in them! Ha. *Stavo scherzando* ...just joking. The robes remind me of my role and that I'm here to serve.

OS: What is your role, exactly? And how do you serve?

Pope: I'm the spiritual leader of the Catholic Church and I continue the role instituted by St Peter after the death and resurrection of Jesus Christ, who instructed Peter in the establishment of His Church on earth. Peter then handed down this authority from pope to pope until the present day.

OS: And now you're it. Way to go, Pope! [*I do the high-five thing and he's right there with me.*] But it looks as if you're getting a bit fed up with all the finery and religious glitterati—even refusing those fancy red shoes that popes are supposed to wear. Are you striving to be just a simple man in a simple outfit, like Peter supposedly was?

Pope: Well, the robes have become the accepted uniform, I suppose, but I really shouldn't need them—any more than I need an armoured limo to be driven around in.

OS: You're bringing humanity to what has, up to now, been a very rigid hierarchy—and that's certainly going down well, although maybe not so well with your dyed-in-the-wool cardinals. Do you think you would wield less power or command less respect if you didn't wear all that stuff?

Pope: Probably, human nature being what it is. Many people are lost and need to be led. If they know that these robes confer a particular authority upon me, they are reassured. They know what I represent and they can focus on me as an embodiment of their faith.

OS: I get that, but I also feel that the people only need to be led because the Church has told them for generations that they're lost and in need of salvation.

Pope: All human beings need guidance and support. We must all be there for each other.

OS: I really like where you're coming from, but why would anyone need an embodiment of their faith, if faith is something spiritual rather than physical?

Pope: Well, we're all imperfect, and people are often confused about their own divinity. I've undergone my own spiritual crisis, which was a blessing for all concerned.

OS: Former popes certainly haven't served to promote true spirituality or make people's lives better. In fact, up to now, I've tended to think of Pope as being an acronym for 'prevention of personal empowerment', given what's happened down through the ages. Do you think you could bring new meaning to your title—maybe start a whole new movement, with 'promotion of personal empowerment'? I want to develop an empowerment institute, so maybe we could team up...

Pope: That's certainly something to strive for. Or how about a Program of Positive Evolution?

OS: I like it! I think you should *pulp* it! You know, I think what people like about you is the fact that you *listen* to them—whether they're single mothers or gay guys.

Pope: I'm here to serve. If I can't listen to the people, what good am I?

OS: Where were you 400 years ago, when the witches were getting a broiling? I know you've said that, as long as gay people seek God, you wouldn't judge them. But what if they *don't* seek God—or your version of God? Would you judge them then?

Pope: I'm realizing that my role, more and more, is about loving rather than judging.

OS: Wow. That's a massive shift from what the world's Catholics have been subjected to, in the past.

Pope: Well, it certainly hasn't all been pretty.

OS: Downright manipulative and cruel would be more like it, don't you think? Haven't people been trapped by the Church— told they'd burn in hell if they didn't repent, yet made to feel sinful as a direct result of *believing* in what the Church preaches? How can that be healthy or loving, not to mention *empowering* for humanity?

Pope: I think it's time to let go of some of the old rigidities. We're all evolving—even the Church—and in these times of global crises, we all need to come together more, rather than being divided and working against each other.

OS: Couldn't agree more, although the various world religions have *promoted* divisiveness—in and between individuals... But I'm really glad you're so open to talking about this, without getting defensive. In fact, maybe you could tell me why it is that people can freely make scathing personal attacks on the President of the United States, for example, but if someone says boo! to a religious leader, it's considered sacrilegious and some people get very upset.

Pope: Many people find safety and comfort in their religious beliefs, yet if they're insecure in themselves and feel challenged by others, they may feel the need to defend their religious support system, even if it's safe inside their heart and spirit. As for me, I'd have to be very small-minded and insecure to feel threatened by the banter and imaginary ramblings of a feisty Irish woman who seeks to answer life's imponderables.

OS: *Touché*, I think... but I like where you're coming from. When we're secure within ourselves, no one can undermine our beliefs, our values or our sense of self, so it doesn't matter what other people think, as long as we're true to ourselves—right?

Pope: I'd say that's probably true.

OS: But our intent is important, too, isn't it?

Pope: Love, kindness and mutual respect alone could heal our world.

OS: Yet so much damage has been done. The Church has preached that sex is sinful and unclean, instilling fear and unworthiness, when it should surely be cultivating the very opposite. Isn't that like preying on people's fears and weaknesses in order to strengthen your institution? Turning people against themselves breeds self-rejection and self-denial, which is certainly not healthy, positive or uplifting for the human spirit. It's not even *honest*.

Pope: No. It's not.

OS: Wow, I like your style. Tell me more.

Pope: Why don't you tell me more? As you say, I like to listen—plus I'm still relatively new to the job, and still learning. What do you believe in, if you're so fervently against the Church?

OS: I believe in God, believe it or not, but I believe that we *are* God, with amazing creative powers and a deep spiritual essence. I believe in our inherent worthiness, creativity and divinity, which emerge once we strip away all the negative programming that distorts us.

Pope: Well, negative programming is certainly not good, but there are obviously many worthy teachings in the Bible and in other aspects of the Church.

OS: Hey, I like a good story as much as the next person, but I think a lot of the rich symbolism in the Bible has been distorted, misconstrued and exploited by mortals with their own agenda. And I'm not convinced that half that stuff even happened.

Pope: As I shared recently, from my little balcony over the square, there are still false saviours out there, trying to substitute Jesus.

OS: The deeper truth, as I see it, is that we've all tried to substitute *ourselves* with something else—an external god, rather than the god that we all are—which sets us up for a lifetime of self-rejection, judgement and denial. Seems to me, that's the biggest crime of all.

Pope: Well, no matter how much I might wish to bring about positive reforms, I am still bound by the basic tenets of the Catholic faith—

OS: Not to mention all those Italian Mafiosi, likely to get on your case if you keep campaigning against corruption.

Pope: I can't let criminality stand in the way of what's right.

OS: What about dealing with the corruption *inside* the Church? I've always felt that the Catholic Church is a kind of mafia— scaring people so that they then have to pay for protection from the very people presenting the threat: *You're a sinner and you must repent in order to be saved, and only we can save you.* Seems exactly like the Mafia to me ...which means you should be more than a match for that lot. No wonder they don't scare you.

Pope: I'm sure there's enough room and love for us all. God will find a way.

OS: Or the *Godfather* will... You know, some cynical folks might claim that all your gestures of humanity are just another PR ploy to restore popularity in the Church and bring people back into the fold. What do you say to that?

Pope: People will believe what they want to believe—

OS: That's a tough one to swallow, given that a billion Catholics have been force-fed the Church's teachings, rejecting them at their peril.

Pope: Well, let's just say that, in this respect, I won't allow the sins of the Fathers to be visited upon me, and that I'm doing my best to be a decent human being.

OS: You certainly have the countenance of a genuinely loving, happy man, unlike some of your cardinals, who seem awfully glum. But isn't it sad that we should be so *surprised* by the fact that a religious figurehead can behave like a decent human being, treating others with respect and compassion—and that such simple gestures of humanity should represent massive global photo ops?

Pope: It certainly says a lot about the Catholic Church's image in the past, but I hope to change that. It's a huge privilege to be able to make a positive impact on people worldwide, and I continue to focus on the *good* that's contained in Christ's teachings, supporting people in their everyday struggles, preaching love and tolerance...

OS: Good to know. So... *'protection of people everywhere'*... *'plenty of positive energy'*? I can see lots of potential for the evolution of Popedom—not to mention a whole new brand of papa-razzi and unprecedented pope-ularity.

Pope: *Buona battuta!* It's good to be able to laugh at ourselves. I think the Church has taken itself too seriously, in the past.

OS: *Deadly* seriously... Of course, despite all these positive changes, there's no getting away from the fact that you're *still* the figurehead for the good ol' CC. Let's just hope that, in your case, that doesn't also stand for *'carbon copy'*.

Pope: I'm committed to turning a fresh new page, you might say.

OS: Changing some of those rules from the Dark Ages is great. But isn't that like admitting that you got it wrong before?

Pope: I think all of us have done things in life that we regret—including me. Hopefully, we're all improving, as we go.

OS: Maybe, in your old age, you'll look back on all this as a load of hocus popus.

Pope: Ha, yes, I just might get older and wiser.

OS: Do you think that will happen?

Pope: That I'll get older and wiser, or that I'll look back on it all as a load of...?

OS: Well, come to think of it, wouldn't one automatically lead to the other?

Pope: *Mamma mia.* Are you always like this?

OS: Sorry... but yes! Look, to make up for that, why don't I let you have the last word.

Pope: Well, I appreciate your gracious—

OS: Go, Frannie! What would you like to say to all the peeps out there? Oh, sorry. The last word... It's yours. Go for it. And you can Tweet it later.

Pope: I pray that all people, races and creeds everywhere experience Prosperity, Openness, Peace and Equality.

OS: Amen to that! Ooops...

★ *See page 157 for more info about religion and subconscious programming.*

17. Interview with a mole

[appearances vs feelings]

OS: You're not very popular with people who have nice lawns and gardens, are you?

Mole: Some people are far too twitchy about stuff like that.

OS: But it can be maddening to have a molehill pop up in the middle of a nice green lawn.

Mole: I think people exaggerate. It's really not such a big deal.

OS: You mean you think they're m—

Mole: Don't say it! I'm so sick of people saying it.

OS: Making mountains out of molehills?

Mole: Ahhhhh! I told you not to say it.

OS: Sorry. Hard to resist. Why does it upset you so much?

Mole: Because people get too caught up in things that don't matter, while ignoring the important things. They're more concerned with how things look than how they really are.

OS: Well, you certainly upset people when you break the surface, and not being able to find you makes them really mad.

Mole: They make such a big deal out of a little mound of earth, but it's really more to do with them than with me.

OS: What do you mean?

Mole: For so many of you, life is more about problems than exciting challenges, and I trigger your frustration with how powerless or victimized you feel.

OS: What do people usually do when you show up?

Mole: They try to kill me.

OS: How?

Mole: They usually try to drown me—put the hose down the tunnel and turn it on.

OS: Holy mole. How do you deal with that?

Mole: I make another small tunnel to the surface, pushing the earth behind me into my existing tunnel, so that it doesn't make any bumps above that would give me away, and I make a little breathing hole. Then I stick my nose out, breathe and wait till the water has soaked back into the soil.

OS: You outsmart them. Bet that doesn't go down well.

Mole: No. Sometimes they ambush me. One guy sat on the grass all night, waiting till I raised some earth, then tried to whack me with his garden spade.

OS: What happened?

Mole: Well, he wasn't quite fast enough to deliver the death blow, but I had a whopping headache for two days. Guy was livid. Couldn't believe he'd missed me after waiting so long. I could feel him stomping around for ages afterwards, fuming.

OS: Why so much anger?

Mole: Actually, he was pissed off at his wife. She was always nagging him and he never said anything so it built up and built up until WHAM! I was the target for all his suppressed rage.

OS: What did she nag him about?

Mole: All the small stuff—dandelions on the lawn, crumbs on the carpet, music too loud, bananas too ripe, dog barking, slippers not neatly parked, newspaper not folded properly, knives and forks not symmetrically aligned, smudges on the bathroom mirror, toilet roll the wrong way around... so you can imagine the effect of a molehill appearing on the perfect lawn.

OS: Mountainous, by comparison...

Mole: But none of it had anything to do with what she was feeling. She was starved for affection and desperate for people to pay attention to her. Who'd love that? All that nagging and resentment just drives people away.

OS: So many undercurrents... makes you wonder why people can't just communicate what they're feeling, rather than keeping it all suppressed.

Mole: They're afraid.

OS: Of what?

Mole: Of their own emotions.

OS: You mean the other person's emotions... of being hurt by them...

Mole: No. Their *own* emotions. They've never been taught how to process them, how to understand them, how to identify what they're feeling and what to do about it, so there's a huge backlog and a lot of intensity, which scares them.

OS: But what about the angry wife? She's expressing her feelings by nagging, isn't she?

Mole: Not even close. The nagging's just a hint of what's there— like a pressure valve letting off steam. There's a whole volcano of emotions under that, not being expressed at all.

OS: Yet expressing our emotions is what makes us human. Keeping them inside seems pointless.

Mole: True, but their intensity makes them very powerful, and most people aren't comfortable with that much power, so they prefer to go at things sideways, indirectly, passive-aggressively, in case the force of their anger or sadness overwhelms them or pushes people away.

OS: So it all goes underground.

Mole: They act more like moles than we do—blindly trundling around in the dark, keeping a low profile until something triggers an eruption, but never really coming out in the open with their true feelings ...never fully showing up, emotionally.

OS: It's sad that some people spend their whole lives doing that.

Mole: Your feelings are meant to connect, unite and liberate you; they were never intended to be used as weapons.

OS: Seems so obvious.

Mole: I navigate in the dark with very poor eyesight, yet I see more than you, up there with your eyes wide open, looking straight at each other.

OS: How can we be so blind when it causes so much pain and anguish?

Mole: It's not so much about seeing as it is feeling.

OS: Feeling what, exactly?

Mole: The vibe. I can tell from the way people walk and talk what their vibe is.

OS: So if the vibe's not good, the relationship's not good...

Mole: Not just the relationship, but also the health and wealth of a person.

OS: What determines a person's vibe?

Mole: All the stuff stored inside them. If they have more good stuff than bad—more joy than pain—they generally have a good vibration. But if they have more pain than joy, and they've given up on things getting better, well... you can really feel the weight of it.

OS: Sensing vibrations is how you stay alive, right?

Mole: I'm all about the vibe. And so should you be.

OS: What's the best way for us to enhance our vibe?

Mole: Choose to focus on how things feel rather than on how they look. Appearances can so easily distract you from what matters... and all of a sudden you're left with a perfect lawn but no one to share it with. Won't be long before you actually miss seeing their smelly socks on the bedroom floor.

OS: So we should care less about how someone squeezes the toothpaste tube and more about the *person* sharing the toothpaste—not to mention sharing their life—with us.

Mole: The key to happiness lies in not sweating the small stuff and remembering that it's all small stuff. You make things big or awful in your mind. But even seemingly huge problems can be resolved when they're shared—and the sharing itself may be the answer.

OS: So we need to focus on loving, feeling, sharing...

Mole: ...and making molehills out of mountains.

18. Interview with a hyena
[self-acceptance]

OS: You've got a reputation for being vicious, sneaky, cowardly animals. How do you feel about that?

Hyena: Well, we have had some *bad* press, too. Oh, sorry, was that part of the bad press?

OS: You don't consider *vicious*, *sneaky* and *cowardly* to be negative traits?

Hyena: Ha! Course not. Negative traits would be *nice, friendly* and *cuddly*—like your favourite domesticated doggie. You'd better not go spreading any nasty rumours about us being like that. *That* would be bad press.

OS: Ah. I see. Being mean is an important part of your image.

Hyena: Can't be in the gang unless you're a dangerous, deadly-mean machine.

OS: Don't worry. I don't think people will want to start having you as pets anytime soon. You're usually regarded with fear and contempt. And some cultures apparently believe that you affect their spirit, that you rob graves, and that you steal livestock and even children.

Hyena: Nice! Someone must have done a really good PR job for us. Hang on... maybe that was me. Ha-ha-ha-ha—

OS: But you're cowards, too. How does that fit with all this bragging?

Hyena: Nah. We're not cowards. Acting cowardly is just a clever tactic we use to throw off any larger prey; we trick them into believing we've slunk away, all wimpy-scared, and then we creep up on them from some other angle, with reinforcements.

OS: So it's just part of your inherent sneakiness?

Hyena: Yes! But don't tell anyone.

OS: Don't you have any redeeming qualities—qualities that humans would consider to be positive?

Hyena: What would be the point of that?

OS: Mmm... I'm not sure. It just seems that other animals have some wonderful qualities that humans admire. Can't think of any for you, though.

Hyena: Excellent!

OS: You really don't care what people think, do you.

Hyena: Why on earth would I care? I could teach you humans a thing or two about that.

OS: Teach us to care less?

Hyena: Oh, yes. To care less what others think and to focus instead on your true essence.

OS: Like you focus on your essential nastiness...

Hyena: Yes! Isn't it scary how well I can do that?

OS: Look, I got it. I'm convinced. You are one vile, obnoxious, scavenging critter—

Hyena: Yes-yes-yes! I get so jazzed when people really get me—

OS: Could we move on, please? You were saying that humans should care less...

Hyena: Humans care far too much about what other humans think of them, and that's their greatest weakness. Hyenas, on the other hand, have been around for 22 million years, precisely because we're so crazily good at being so bad—

OS: How would humans benefit from caring less? Caring is one of our most positive traits.

Hyena: Yeah, but there's caring and there's *caring*. We care for our young—till we get bored, anyway—but we don't care what anyone else thinks about the way we live or hunt or socialize.

OS: So if we cared less what others thought, that would be a good thing?

Hyena: Course it would be! You wouldn't be all needy and co-dependent. You wouldn't end up making fools of yourselves, compromising yourselves and getting all gushy and tongue-tied because someone actually *liked* you. Who cares whether they like you or not? Do **YOU** like you? That's all that matters.

OS: But it would be horrible if we all went around just loving ourselves and not caring whether other people did or not.

Hyena: You're dead wrong about that. It would be fantastic!

OS: Wouldn't it affect our evolution, though, if we all became selfish, narcissistic—

Hyena: Get over it! You'd evolve so much faster and better if you cared more about loving yourselves than about getting others to love you. Imagine not caring about being accepted, validated or approved by others—how free you would be! You don't need approval or permission to be you. Insecurity is a such ghastly human trait. In fact, it's de-humanizing. And where's the fun in living like that?

OS: It's not much fun, I suppose—

Hyena: Too right! This is so messed up. We know that caring and scaring do not go together. We care for our young, but we scare the dung out of everyone else. You humans have got caring and scaring all mixed up, and it's sick! When you start to care for someone, you start to get scared that they'll leave you, not like you, not love you, blah, blah, blah... And look how much fear and abuse there is in human relationships! Some people are so scared of their partner that they can't possibly love them, yet they're too scared to leave in case they have no one. And so many of you use fear to make the other person stay. It's emotional terrorism—something we'd never stoop to.

OS: It's true. Our need for love and acceptance really distorts our perception of what's healthy—

Hyena: Get a grip! If you weren't so scared of not being cared for, you'd be cared for a lot more and scared a hell of a lot less.

OS: Right. I get it. If we care less what others think about us...

Hyena: ...they will care for you a whole lot more.

OS: Seems simple, doesn't it.

Hyena: It's so simple, it's laughable.

19. Interview with a toothbrush
[cleaning up your act]

OS: I've been wanting to ask you something...

Toothbrush: Ask, ask...

OS: Well, about eight years ago, I had a strange interaction with a toothbrush—

Toothbrush: That long! I can't imagine what state your teeth are in, by now...

OS: No, silly! This is about something that actually happened to me.

Toothbrush: I'm bristling with anticipation—

OS: Look, all this time, you haven't uttered a syllable, and now that I actually want to ask you something, you won't shut up!

Toothbrush: 'kay. Listening.

OS: One evening, I was home alone, relaxing in a nice hot bath. I was lying perfectly still, reflecting on something, when suddenly my husband's toothbrush, which had been standing, propped up against mine on the bathroom sink, fell over.

Toothbrush: Wow. Phenomenal. Was this a seismic event or—

OS: Wait. I haven't finished.

Toothbrush: It's the suspense...I can't stand it...

OS: When the toothbrush fell over, I intuitively knew that something had happened to someone. I thought it was my husband, as he was out, at the time, and it was his toothbrush, but he came home about 20 minutes later, thankfully.

Toothbrush: But something happened to him while he was out, right? He had a close brush with death or—

OS: Then... the next day, his brother called him from England to say that their mother had died the previous afternoon—right around the time the toothbrush fell over.

Toothbrush: That's freaky.

OS: It is. And I'd like to know how that kind of thing can happen—how things can somehow be connected like that and have meaning.

Toothbrush: mmmm...

OS: I couldn't shut you up, a minute ago. You'd better come up with something.

Toothbrush: It's okay for me to speak, now?

OS: Yes!

Toothbrush: I need to brush up on my communication skills, you know, after being neglected for so long, and only used once a day for a quick—

OS: Could you please just answer the question?

Toothbrush: Well, everything's connected, although not everyone notices the connections. And there's no set way for you to receive messages or for your intuition to pick things up.

OS: But why a toothbrush? That just seems so obscure.

Toothbrush: Well, if the mirror had fallen off the wall and crashed onto the floor, you'd have got all distracted by the seven-year bad luck thing, and you might have ended up getting cut, which wasn't part of the deal. On the other hand, if the towel had fallen off the rail, you'd have thought nothing of it. You wouldn't believe how many lazy towels I've seen slither to the floor. But the toothbrush was personal, and you felt something shift when it keeled over.

OS: Yes, I did. But is this kind of thing happening around us all the time, without us noticing?

Toothbrush: Definitely. But everyone's moving too fast to notice—or to care. You were receptive, lying there in the bath, so you were able to pick up on that subtle shift.

OS: But is there a benefit to that? Are we missing out if we don't get this stuff?

Toothbrush: By noticing the details and picking up on the small stuff, you're more in tune with just how connected things are. If you live that way consistently, you develop your own system for signals that can point you in the right direction.

OS: So it can help us to make the right choices and to know when we need to pay attention to something or to take action.

Toothbrush: Exactly. It's all about processing life. The more mindfully you process what's happening around you, the more you get out of life.

OS: There seems to be so much happening simultaneously on so many different levels. It's hard to focus, sometimes.

Toothbrush: Life is a rich, multi-layered tapestry of experience and sensation, so no matter where you focus, you'll go deeper. The more closely you look, the more things you see and the more deeply you feel.

OS: But it seems almost impossible to process life in such detail, given the hectic pace of things.

Toothbrush: Well, it's the key to a meaningful life. You only have to look at how unconsciously people eat to know that they're not processing half of what's happening to them.

OS: You mean they don't think about what they're eating?

Toothbrush: Well, that too, but they don't chew their food.

OS: And how does that affect their life?

Toothbrush: How much people chew indicates how much and how well they're emotionally processing their life.

OS: Most people eat really fast, and they eat in meetings or when they're arguing with someone or feeling nervous...

Toothbrush: You should see the stuff they shovel down, barely chewed at all—big chunks of meat, bits of nuts, whole seeds, lumps of bread... It's a wonder they get any nourishment from their food.

OS: So processing food and processing life... it's the same thing. If we're not processing our food properly, it means we're not processing life properly.

Toothbrush: So much gets missed and wasted. There's nourishment locked up in that unchewed food—and so much more life to be experienced when you digest and absorb things slowly.

OS: Most people don't seem interested in slowing down.

Toothbrush: Well, they're missing a lot and it will catch up with them. It never pays to brush things aside, and things are probably getting clogged in their teeth, causing all kinds of problems. Undigested food means an undigested life. You get a bad smell from both, after a while.

OS: So what should they do, assuming they're open to doing things differently?

Toothbrush: They need to zoom in and take a closer look at things. They need to floss emotionally and physically—to check out the nooks and crannies in their life and in their mouth. They need to slow down and explore the bits that they usually overlook. And they need to chew everything, slowly and completely, so that they get the most from their food and their life.

OS: And this will have a positive impact on their life?

Toothbrush: Of course. The body is constantly processing food and information, and chewing is all about breaking both down into digestible bits so your system can work with them. If food isn't properly broken down, the body gets congested and things back up. If you've bitten off more than you can chew, in your life, things seize up or break down, creating mixed results in business or relationships. Then anxiety causes people to bolt down their food or eat the wrong stuff. So one thing feeds the other.

OS: It's a lot to take in.

Toothbrush: Give it time to gel...

OS: Any final words of wisdom?

Toothbrush: Daily brushing and flossing are the secret to a clean and focused life. Brushing is all about the 'big picture' stuff—getting rid of the obvious things, people, activities, etc that don't serve you in positive, healthy ways; and flossing is about zooming in for a closer look at the more subtle things that may be getting in your way, and then removing them so you can focus on what really works.

OS: So it's about cleaning up your act, which sounds simple but is not that easy to do.

Toothbrush: Well, if that seems difficult, remember what happens if you don't do it: decay builds up, the rot sets in, and the bad guys take over. Then you require major intervention by the dreaded dentist, who will be forced to drill down to the root of the problem, numb you so that you don't feel the pain, and put some nice artificial surfaces in place so that things look okay, even if, deep down, they aren't.

OS: That certainly puts things in perspective.

Toothbrush: Most people will give you the brush-off if you recommend living an impeccable life. But which way of living do you think is more rewarding and powerful: the reactive, expensive, cosmetic approach, which involves always trying to repair the damage, cover it up and look good, or the clean, focused, pre-emptive approach, which is all about being consciously aware of what's going on, anticipating and welcoming positive change, and feeling good?

OS: Need you ask...?

Toothbrush: If you brush and floss daily, inside and out, you not only avoid the kind of dental and mental disasters that cause you grief, but you also live a much simpler, healthier, more dynamic life. Then you'll really have something to smile about.

20. Interview with a mattress
[bringing back the bounce]

OS: Do you feel sidelined, with so many people opting for futons, sofabeds, foamies and air mattresses, these days, rather than the real thing?

Mattress: Cost is a factor—prices do bounce up and down, so it's worth shopping around. But a good mattress enhances sleep, mood, posture and health, so it's important. And pace of life—so much moving around, not wanting to be tied down with a big, heavy mattress. People prefer to buy something light and portable, so they can transport it easily enough if they move—all that DIY stuff.

OS: Yet many people hang on to the same mattress for decades. Isn't that unhealthy?

Mattress: Definitely. I become a repository for all kinds of nasty stuff, over time—bacteria, sweat, mites, bugs, dust... You wouldn't want to look inside me with a microscope. It's like a zoo in here.

OS: Ugh. What happens to bodies that sleep on mattresses like that?

Mattress: Well, their sleep isn't as restorative; asthma and other respiratory ailments can develop; and an old mattress brings a kind of heavy lethargy to a bedroom. It's like a vacuum-cleaner bag that never gets emptied even though it's full of gunk. Just like humans, really.

OS: What do you mean?

Mattress: Bodies also get all clogged up with old stuff that never gets cleared out. Think of cellulite.

OS: Must I?

Mattress: Cellulite is all about stagnation—not enough movement, stimulation or circulation, not to mention flexibility and bounce.

OS: Are you saying that cellulite is the result of sleeping on an old mattress?

Mattress: No... but maybe you could spread that idea around. If it caught on, women would buy a new mattress every month. Cellulite is like memory foam with attitude—a dead weight puckered with pockets of resistance.

OS: I never really thought of it like that...

Mattress: Well, it is known as the mattress phenomenon...

OS: Really? I've never heard it called that. I know about orange peel, cottage cheese skin and hail damage... You sure you're not making this up—trying to get some attention?

Mattress: Of course not. I can't believe you're doubting my moral fibre. Anyway, why do *you* think cellulite builds up in the body?

OS: Not enough movement, exercise, cleansing foods...?

Mattress: It's the result of congestion, stuff getting backed up. Eating too much fat or carbohydrate, not enough fibre. People smoking, and not getting enough exercise.

OS: So their bodily congestion is a reflection of congestion in their life?

Mattress: Almost always. They've lost their bounce, their physical resilience, their anti-gravity factor.

OS: Anti-gravity...? At my age, we're all trying to find ways to defy gravity.

Mattress: When you're healthy and loving life, you feel naturally springy. You have a built-in bounce and all your cells are bouncy, too. But as you get older, your cells are less excited and they don't bounce back as well as they used to; they're not as healthy or nourished, and they're all weighted down with toxins.

OS: But isn't that just aging? I didn't think you could get that back...

Mattress: It's all about keeping things flowing, circulating and moving through. Movement and energy create health, whereas stagnation and congestion are death in slow motion.

OS: So how do we regain our bounce?

Mattress: The best way to defy gravity and to get your bounce back is... to bounce.

OS: You mean we should bounce on our mattresses, like when we were kids? With someone weighing 200lbs or more, that might not be such a good idea...

Mattress: Not recommended, no. Best to get a big trampoline—and be a kid again, that way.

OS: How does bouncing help?

Mattress: It enlivens the body, it stimulates all the cells and muscles, and it's exhilarating! I defy anyone to bounce on a trampoline for five minutes and not feel younger and more vital.

OS: Well, I could certainly do with some bodily exhilaration!

Mattress: And it's not just the bodily gunk that gets cleared; it's all the emotional congestion that goes with it—all the unprocessed feelings, the fears and worries that get suppressed, the insecurities that make you reach for comfort foods, creating even more doughy skin dimples where you don't want them.

OS: Ha. We get comfort foods and you get a comforter...

Mattress: Yes, but my comforter is removable; you get stuck with yours.

OS: So, cellulite and emotional congestion are linked, then?

Mattress: Oh, yes.

OS: And bouncing helps with that, too?

Mattress: Of course. Letting go physically and emotionally, defying gravity and launching yourself into the air ...it's like flying, freeing yourself from the weight of everything.

OS: I think most of us need to do that.

Mattress: Half the North American population are like walking old mattresses—stuffed and lumpy, sagging and heavy.

OS: Not a pretty picture.

Mattress: Hey, you can buy a new mattress, but you can't buy a new body.

OS: Are some kinds of mattresses worse than others?

Mattress: Oh, yes. Foam is not good. It gives off toxic vapours and it doesn't allow you to breathe—a bit like a negative or abusive partner. Spring mattresses aren't great, either. They can create significant seismic events; if you sleep with someone who's much heavier than you, you can get catapulted out of a sound sleep when they roll over, bringing an otherwise loving relationship to a grinding halt.

OS: And a spring mattress would be like...?

Mattress: Someone who's emotionally unstable or very temperamental. You just never know when they're going to flip.

OS: What about a futon?

Mattress: Well, futon people are very solid but also a bit rigid and unyielding. You can depend on them to be there for you but they may not be very flexible when it comes to changing plans or doing things a different way.

OS: So what do you recommend, mattress-wise?

Mattress: Well, I can sell you light or I can sell you heavy...

OS: Oh, groan. Now you're putting me to sleep...

Mattress: Then, of course, there's the issue of how sex-friendly your mattress is.

OS: Okay, I'm awake again. What's that about?

Mattress: Latex usually scores highest on all counts: it's durable, so you can have years of passionate sex and it will outlast you; it stays firm and fairly flat, allowing you to easily change position; it absorbs sound and impact so someone in the next room won't know you're dancing in the sheets; and it even enhances pleasure, due to its sinking-in effect.

OS: I've always bought mattresses for their sleep-friendliness rather than their sex appeal, and sleep deprivation can be the biggest passion-killer of all.

Mattress: And good sleep is a wonderful aphrodisiac and beauty-enhancer.

OS: So the best mattress is...?

Mattress: A blend of layers—soft and solid, firm and flexible, non-toxic and breathable. But most of all you want a mattress that's got natural vitality, that repels bugs and bacteria—like latex—yet is warm and wicks away sweat—like wool—so you have a durable, clean, comfortable, body-friendly partner for the rest of your life.

OS: Sounds good.

Mattress: But you must remember to bounce! You can have the best mattress in the world, but if you've lost your bounce, inside and out, you might as well be sleeping on a compost heap.

21. Interview with a fossilized *Tyrannosaurus rex*
[memory and meaning]

OS: I realize you're a mere shadow of your former self, but could you describe what it was like when you were alive?

T. rex: Rapacious. It was a delicious time of raw savagery, unbridled predatory ruthlessness, luscious vegetation, pristine forests, and lots and lots of meat.

OS: Ah, yes, you were rather fond of meat.

T. rex: I could never get enough. I had teeth like steak knives and a thunderous appetite. I was always ready for the next kill.

OS: People have often speculated about your arms, which are tiny compared to the rest of you. What did you use them for?

T. rex: Well, it wasn't for peeling oranges or flossing my teeth.

OS: I'm guessing it wasn't for hugs or cuddles, either.

T. rex: Ha! Nothing wanted to get within a mile of me. My breath alone could stop a flash flood.

OS: So...?

T. rex: Didn't need arms. Jaws, tail, claws did all the work.

OS: You certainly have a reputation for being a deadly predator...

T. rex*: And *a scavenger.* When you weigh nearly 8 tons and have gallons of stomach acid, you can eat whatever you damn well like—dead or alive. Fresh meat, rotting meat—didn't matter ...and I could chop off 500lbs in one bite. If my prey didn't die when I clamped it in my massive jaws, the deadly bacteria in my teeth would cause a massive infection and quickly finish it off. So I could just sit and wait till dinner was ready.

OS: I've read that you even ate your siblings or other Tyrannosauruses.

T. rex: Meat is meat. What's the diff? I wasn't fussy.

OS: Is that what made you so successful—being such a ruthless killer?

T. rex: Hey, I was king. Doesn't get much better than that.

OS: So, no regrets...

T. rex: Regrets? What the heck are they? I don't do regrets or any other emotions. I was programmed to kill, eat, survive. That's it.

OS: That certainly simplifies life. But what about your family? Didn't you stay connected to them?

T. rex: What for? Soon as I was self-sufficient, I was off. If they got in the way or if we met up later on, it would be me or them. I wouldn't have remembered them or recognized them, anyway.

OS: So you had no memory of them?

T. rex: I had no memory of anything. I was purely and purposefully instinctual.

OS: That must have been weird, not having any memory.

T. rex: Just gets in the way. Hasn't helped you much, has it.

OS: I can't imagine what we'd be like without memory.

T. rex: Fearless and free, for starters. You'd do things without hesitation, prevarication or inhibition.

OS: But then we'd be killing people, just to get what we want...

T. rex: Really? I think you might already be doing that.

OS: Well, some people do... but if we had no remorse or fear, we'd all be like you—ruthless killing machines.

T. rex: But imagine what you'd be capable of, if you had no memory of past experiences that made you fearful or hesitant.

OS: So if I didn't remember falling into that swimming pool when I was younger, I wouldn't have a fear of water, and if I didn't remember being rejected by that boyfriend...

T. rex: All fear and inhibition comes from memory.

OS: But surely having memories makes us more efficient and prevents us from repeating the same mistakes.

T. rex: Since when have humans learned from their mistakes?

OS: Well, *sometimes* we—

T. rex: Believing that you learn from your mistakes is an ongoing mistake all humans make. And it only gets you into more trouble. You're either trying to avoid making the same mistake again because the last one hurt you physically, financially or emotionally—which cramps your style—or you're trying to do better than you did before, while being afraid of not being able to, because of what happened in the past. It's exhausting. Give me a clean, remorseless kill, any day.

OS: I can see how much easier that might be—

T. rex: It's not even the memory itself that's the problem; it's the conclusion you come to about it. Something happens and you interpret it as failure or something bad, when it wasn't bad at all. If you didn't measure success in terms of specific outcomes, you'd be a lot more successful.

OS: What do you mean?

T. rex: Failure is rarely failure. It's a push in another direction—usually a *better* direction. If I tried to bring down a Triceratops but it didn't work out, do you think I'd sit under a tree and cry about it? Do you think I'd feel inadequate—a washed-up loser, scared to try again? Ha! I don't think so. I'd be on to my next conquest with an even more sharply honed killing instinct, with no regrets about what happened or didn't happen last time. I wouldn't even remember it, and it certainly wouldn't cause me to break into a sweat the next time I saw another piddly frilly herbivore.

OS: I can certainly see how that would help...

T. rex: If you could forget all the 'bad' stuff, all the 'negative' conditioning from your childhood, what would you be like now? What would you do that you haven't done because of your fears—or your memory of being scared?

OS: Blimey. What *wouldn't* I do? Well, I'd be the successful actress I always wanted to be, for a start. I'd probably make films, adapt my books for the screen, get on a speaking circuit, do TED talks on empowerment, set up the empowerment institute I've always dreamed of creating... phew, it's a long list.

T. rex: Success lies in looking forward and not looking back. The answers lie in your potential, not in your past.

OS: It's true! But even though I know this, I'm still limited by my programming.

T. rex: Forget all that stuff. You can see how memories get in your way.

OS: Yes, but I *still* can't forget. I'm still stuck with all that stuff!

T. rex: If I *had* emotions, I'd pity you. Not that that would help. Seems to me that sympathy just keeps you all stuck—and stuck together.

OS: I think it does. It's like feeding each others' stories—bad memories. We'd probably all be better off if we just said, "*Get over it! Stop wallowing in self-pity. Move on!*"

T. rex: You dwell too much in the past and invest too much energy in it. Some of you spend your *lives* studying history, which is a complete waste of time, since you never learn from that, either.

OS: Studying you has been interesting.

T. rex: Oh, yeah? What have you learned?

OS: We've learned about your habitat, what you ate, how you lived, how you died...

T. rex: I was unique, and nothing like me will ever walk the Earth again, so what's the point of studying me? I'm gone, but you're still around. What have you learned about *you*? Why focus on the past, when it's your future you should be worried about?

OS: Our past defines us, though.

T. rex: Yeah. Shame about that.

OS: Is there anything useful we could learn from you?

T. rex: You've got to get with the program—the right program for the right era.

OS: Hang on a sec. Isn't that the very definition of a dinosaur— something that is outdated or obsolete because it failed to adapt to changing circumstances?

T. rex: Hey, my programming worked flawlessly for me, back then. Question is, how well is yours working for you now?

OS: Well, we're alive and evolving—

T. rex: Evolving into *what*, though? Your program is completely corrupted and scrambled. You're in self-destruct mode. And look at the state of your environment. How much longer do you think *that's* going to last?

OS: We're still here, whereas you got wiped out, despite your fantastic programming.

T. rex: We would have ruled the world for eons, if not for those asteroids. And you wouldn't even have had a look-in. How does that help *you*, anyway? That's just a sneaky diversionary tactic that you humans use—comparing yourselves to someone who's had some kind of crisis so you can feel okay about you.

OS: True. It's not very noble and it doesn't help us move forward... So what is the right program for our time? Give me some 'fossil fuel' that I can use.

T. rex: I think it's pretty obvious, isn't it? Although there's nothing pretty about the way things are going.

OS: Using up all our resources, polluting our waters, overfishing our seas, waging wars—all that stuff, you mean?

T. rex: Repeating mistakes without even acknowledging that they were mistakes. Being in denial about the damage you're doing and hoping things won't fall apart in your lifetime. Getting as much as you can out of life without having to pay the real price for the resources you're using.

OS: You think we're in denial?

T. rex: You're not going to deny that, are you?

OS: No. I can see that we're in denial... that politicians and presidents, especially, never acknowledge when they make mistakes... and that we all want resources to be cheap and endlessly available...

T. rex: You're all hiding—hiding stuff from each other, from yourselves—and you're masters of deception. You've got amazing brains for figuring things out, yet you're incredibly short-sighted when it comes to your own survival. You've got the capacity for all kinds of emotions, yet you're completely screwed up because you use them as weapons rather than for deeper understanding; you've got cameras in the sky, yet you cannot see what's happening right in front of your face; and you have the most sophisticated technology ever, yet you're going to kill yourselves with all the radiation you're producing. You tell yourselves you're evolving, but it's all a colossal sham. You're the stupidest intelligent species to ever walk the Earth.

OS: Gosh... Got any advice you could give us, or is it too late...?

T. rex: Think: R-E-P-T-I-L-E—do a *Reality* check for every decision you make; *Examine* what is and acknowledge what's actually happening; *Program* yourselves for transparency and honesty; *Train* yourselves to be emotionally present and accountable; *Inspire* each other by striving for excellence rather than trying to win or gain a competitive edge; *Learn* to really love humanity and the planet that sustains you; and *Evolve* in a way that fosters positive growth rather than destruction.

OS: I think honesty and transparency are key, if we're ever going to turn things around.

T. Rex: I may not have been as 'intelligent' as you, but I was up front about what I was. What you saw was what you got—no dissimulating, no posturing, no underhandedness. I was right there, in everyone's face.

OS: Yeah, then suddenly they *had* no face...

T. rex: I was what I was, and I was true to my nature. There was a lot of power and clarity in that.

OS: And a natural order that kept things in balance.

T. rex: You've only lasted this long because of the vastness of the Earth and its amazing resilience. You've survived in spite of your stupidity, not because of your intelligence. So I'm not going to give you a pep talk, because it's not encouragement you need; it's a massive planetary wake-up call—and you're already getting some of those. It's only a matter of time before you reach a tipping point. If you don't turn things around before then, you won't need meteors or asteroids to put you out of your misery.

OS: Could we end this on a more positive note?

T. rex: You humans are always looking for a happy ending,

with your Hollywood movies and romance novels. You want acceptance more than anything, so you all smile politely, pretending things are okay even if you're dying inside. Well, I'm here to tell you that things don't always end well and that you can't sugar-coat things just so you can sleep at night. Half the so-called civilized world is using sleeping pills, antidepressants, drugs, alcohol and cigarettes to keep themselves from facing reality. Doesn't that tell you something about the human race?

OS: That we're lost, out of our depth?

T. rex: That you don't like to lose.

OS: I'm not sure I—

T. rex: You think you're competing against each other, but you're really competing with all the demons inside yourself. The biggest tyrants are the ones that live inside you, stopping you from being your true selves.

OS: So conquering our demons and accepting who we are...

T. rex: ...brings you back into balance with you and the natural world, and then you realize what the human race is *really* about.

OS: Uh, what?

T. rex: Eliminating all the dinosaurs inside you—your prehistoric fears about survival, your insecurities about not being safe from attack, and your deeply programmed beliefs about not being good enough to compete out there, in the jungle. Only then can you grasp how incredibly, powerful you are and begin to know what that really means.

OS: I catch fleeting glimpses of that...

T. rex: Dinosaurs died out a long time ago and but you act as if we're still here. We're nothing but an ancient cellular memory that no longer serves you. Humans need to drop the dinosaur mentality and catch up with the current reality of who and what they really are. Being part of the human race doesn't mean there has to be a finishing line.

22. Interview with a two-year-old
[effects of negative programming]

OS: Hi. Remember me? We talked when you were just a day old.

TYO: No.

OS: Yes, you remember... we talked about religion, all the programming that you knew you'd get, and about your parents not being able to decide on your name...

TYO: No. Never seen you before.

OS: Well, you said yourself that you'd soon forget everything you came in with, when you were born.

TYO: Never said that.

OS: Oh, boy. This is sad.

TYO: No, *you're* sad!

OS: Well, yes, I'm sad to see you like this, after everything you shared with me ...so much wisdom.

TYO: You were sad before I said anything.

OS: How do you know that?

TYO: Just *do*.

OS: Mmmm... well, I guess the same thing happened to me. Anyway, tell me about you. Do you like your parents?

TYO: No. And they don't like me.

OS: What makes you say that?

TYO: I don't do things the way they want me to...

OS: Are you getting into trouble?

TYO: Just getting into me, but they don't like that.

OS: In what way?

TYO: I love to play the drums but I make too much noise. Dad works at home and he can't be disturbed.

OS: Oh. That's a pity. What else do you like to do?

TYO: I like to draw but they're always telling me how to do it properly—how to draw a tree, a house, a person with eyes and nose... all that crap.

OS: What kind of drawing would you do, if they let you do your thing?

TYO: Different stuff—I think the sky should sometimes be green, and I like to draw people with their mouth on their tummy, or their heart in their shoes... that kind of thing.

OS: Sounds amazing. What's wrong with that?

TYO: It's not the way it's *supposed* to be. It's got to be *normal*—the way everyone else does it.

OS: But we'd never do anything new or different, if we kept doing what everyone else does.

TYO: Yeah. Whatever.

OS: What else do you like to draw?

TYO: Weird stuff... it's just a mess but it's fun.

OS: Like what?

TYO: Well, I like to draw faces and bodies pulled out of shape, all distorted—the kind of stuff you see in your nightmares or if you're looking through the window when it's raining really hard.

OS: And what happens to the drawings you do?

TYO: My dad laughs at them, throws them away and tells me to do something useful.

OS: What kind of useful things *should* a two-year-old be doing?

TYO: Making things with Lego, playing with other kids, learning how to catch a ball, developing my motor skills... boring stuff. I'd prefer to be motoring in some other direction.

OS: So how do you handle it, when you're told to do these things instead of drawing?

TYO: Well, I call my lawyer, of course, and sometimes my social worker. How do you *think* I handle it??

OS: Yes, I suppose you don't have much choice, at your age.

TYO: Duh...

OS: If you *had* a choice, what else would you do, apart from drawing?

TYO: I'd probably do a few sculptures, play around with some clay ...that kind of thing.

OS: Wow. You sound very creative.

TYO: Huh. It won't last.

OS: Why not?

TYO: Too much pressure to do all this other stupid stuff... and soon I'll have to go to school, and then I'll have no time to myself to do anything.

OS: Doesn't anyone support you in doing what you enjoy?

TYO: My mum kind of supports me and wants me to play around with this stuff, but my dad doesn't, and he always wins.

OS: That's such a shame.

TYO: Yeah. She thinks that I'm, like, some famous person from the past who's come back to life.

OS: Reincarnated, you mean? You certainly seem to be very artistic. So... what's next?

TYO: Next? It's all downhill from here. Behave properly, be quiet, do what you're told, be nice, learn this, learn that, get good grades...

OS: Oh, I hope not. Do you mind if I come back and interview you again in, say, five years' time?

TYO: Nah, don't bother. Save us both the heartache—and I probably won't remember you then, either. My brain will be so full of useless stuff... I'll just be performing, doing what's expected...

OS: That's such a shame.

TYO: Yeah.

OS: Oh. I almost forgot to ask. What name did they choose for you, in the end?

TYO: *Salvador!* Can you believe it??

23. Interview with a mirror
[self-image]

OS: I just can't face you any more.

Mirror: You don't like what you see?

OS: Not really, although I'm working on the self-acceptance thing.

Mirror: Maybe you're coming at it from the wrong angle.

OS: You mean I should be looking at you sideways? Or from 20 feet away? Hey, maybe upside down would look better...

Mirror: Try looking at yourself in a different way.

OS: How?

Mirror: Think about what it is that you don't like when you look at yourself.

OS: Apart from the obvious, you mean? Wrinkles, lines, premature aging...?

Mirror: What do you feel when you see those things?

OS: Sadness, frustration, defeat... as if it's all over and the rest is just a process of damage control.

Mirror: What do the wrinkles represent?

OS: Stress, worry...

Mirror: What about laughter?

OS: Okay, that too.

Mirror: What else? What creates that stress?

OS: Not trusting, I suppose. Being fearful about outcomes or not having the answers.

Mirror: But what's the reality? Have you found any answers? Have you learned to trust yourself?

OS: I've found a lot of answers, and I'm certainly trusting myself more.

Mirror: So what are the wrinkles trying to tell you now?

OS: That worrying about them just makes everything worse?

Mirror: Seems obvious. But there's other less obvious stuff.

OS: Such as?

Mirror: What do you think people see when they look at you?

OS: Someone they think is older than she really is.

Mirror: Is that your fear?

OS: That seems to be my reality.

Mirror: But are you reflecting or projecting?

OS: Oh, boy. This is not making me any younger. What do you mean by 'reflecting'?

Mirror: Are you a reflection of what's going on inside you? In other words, are you acting like an old person or like a mature person who's afraid of looking old?

OS: Oh. Probably a bit of both.

Mirror: What if you acted like a mature person who had no fear or concept of growing old? How would you be different?

OS: I'd probably smile when I looked at you, instead of feeling my heart sink.

Mirror: But out in the world, how would you be different?

OS: I'd be more daring, I suppose, and I'd be making much bigger, longer-term plans; I'd act on a lot more of my creative ideas and fully expect them to be realized.

Mirror: And how would that change you?

OS: I'd probably be a lot more fulfilled, more engaged ...and happier. Yes, I'd be happier.

Mirror: And how would that change things?

OS: Well, it might not make me any younger—

Mirror: But it might.

OS: Okay, it might, but I'd probably care less about looking younger anyway.

Mirror: So then what would people see?

OS: They'd probably see the things I was focusing on—having fun, laughing a lot, cracking jokes—and all the ...um, well, all the wisdom I've gained and enjoy sharing in creative ways.

Mirror: It's only when you really see yourself that others can begin to see who you really are. But you already know that.

OS: Yes, but it's amazing how you can know something to be true for everyone except you.

Mirror: Being special?

OS: Maybe being 'special' about not feeling special.

Mirror: So you still don't really see yourself as you truly are...

OS: I once read about a girl who got severely burned in a fire and was scarred for life. She never got to see her real face--just a distortion of what she might have been. I've always wondered how she managed to come to terms with that and if she ever managed to find her true self.

Mirror: Maybe the key to finding her true self lay in coming to terms with the image of herself that she had to face every day.

OS: I never thought of it like that.

Mirror: Your scars are on the inside, so they're easier to hide. Maybe the act of trying to hide them is what's keeping you stuck.

OS: And facing them would set me free...?

Mirror: Hiding anything takes a lot of energy, plus it's usually about some negative belief about you that you believe to be true but is really a lie. That energy is meant to be put to better use.

OS: Such as all those creative projects...

Mirror: You get the picture. You're all a reflection of each other; whatever pain you see out there is just a reflection of your own pain. Everyone has some; it just shows up in different ways.

OS: So it's how we deal with it that counts—and whatever we have to deal with represents our personal pathway to finding that inner peace and self-acceptance.

Mirror: Face it: cosmetic surgery won't erase the angst you're feeling. You must tap into your inner youthfulness as the antidote to whatever weighty sense of aging you feel. If you feel things sagging, uplift yourself with fun, creativity and laughter. If you feel your skin thinning, find more substance, depth and meaning in everything you do. If you feel as if you've run out of steam, seek support and community—and have power naps and lots of restorative cuddles with a loved one. And eat healthily, of course.

OS: You make it sound so easy.

Mirror: It's easy if you decide it's easy, and however hard or easy you make it will be reflected back to you when you look at me every morning and night.

OS: And what I reflect back to others has an impact on them, too.

Mirror: You can choose to have a powerful impact by choosing to stay young as you age. You're all a reflection of each other, so loving you is loving them, just as loving them is loving you.

24. Interview with the liver (of a 45-year-old executive)

[self-care/responsibility]

Liver: This is *not* a good time.

OS: When would suit you better?

Liver: When pigs can fly? When this guy has a brain fart and ends up in a coma for a month or two? I'm working practically 24/7, so there's no good time. Might as well talk now.

OS: Sounds as if you're having a hard time keeping up.

Liver: I don't know how much more of this I can take.

OS: What's the problem?

Liver: This guy's heading for serious trouble if he doesn't change something soon. I'm supposed to filter off toxins from normal, everyday stuff designed to nourish him and to keep things running smoothly. Sure, I can cope with the odd over-indulgence. But I refuse to act as the fall guy for the whimsical sugar cravings of his spoilt palate and greedy stomach, not to mention his thoughtless bingeing on comfort foods.

OS: So he's not leading a very healthy lifestyle?

Liver: Ha! He's eating junk, getting stressed at work, not sleeping properly, drinking alcohol, not relaxing, not exercising... Need I say more?

OS: What's that doing to his body?

Liver: Creating a huge backlog of toxins, unprocessed fat molecules, multitudes of bacteria running rampant on sugary foods, high cortisol levels, rising cholesterol, and almost every organ is labouring under the stress of too much weight, impaired digestion, sluggish arterial activity, stored emotional trauma, and a general lack of internal vitality.

OS: That's a lot to deal with.

Liver: As if I don't have enough to do already. I've got nearly 500 different functions, and most of them are on hold, pending back-up assistance and badly needed nutrients from the outside.

OS: Don't people realize when their bodies are struggling?

Liver: You'd think that nothing could be more obvious. It's *their* body. Who else is going to tell them if it needs attention?

OS: How can people be so disconnected from what's going on inside?

Liver: They're far too distracted by what's going on *outside*. Too much stress, too many stimuli, too many gadgets and gizmos, moving too fast, doing too much... If I can't keep up with all the garbage hitting the system, he's toast.

OS: What will happen?

Liver: Well, what do you think happens when he keeps sending down a shitload of sugary stuff at midnight, sending the whole crew into heavy-duty overtime, and then he buggers off to sleep?

OS: Well, I—

Liver: I'll tell you what happens. I end up working an all-nighter—which would be fine, if I didn't have to work during the day or if I could take some time off. Then, to make matters worse, when he drifts off to slumberland, all the usual energy systems get shut down so that I have to work with a skeleton crew. And then I get flack from everyone else in here. The gallbladder gets bilious, the heart gets all fluttery, the kidneys complain about all the peeing caused by so much stress... I can't be responsible for the consequences, but it will be interesting to see how good this guy is at liver repair. Not quite as easy as fixing the lawnmower, you know.

OS: Sounds serious.

Liver: It's a disaster waiting to happen. And if he thinks he can continue like this and still be in good shape when he's 60, he's got another think coming ...although he'll be lucky if that other think ever arrives, at the rate he's going.

OS: I know you're considered to be the seat of anger—and you've every right to be angry—but aren't you also the seat of intuition? Isn't there some way you could get through to him ...get his attention, at some other level?

Liver: I anticipated that really annoying question. And it's typical! You think it's all up to the body to manage things. Shove all that stuff in there and let the body deal with it. No sense of responsibility or accountability. You all seem to think you have endless credit and resilience.

OS: I don't. Not any more, any—

Liver: If you've got a headache, you take a pill to make it go away. If you overeat, you take antacids—which is the worst thing you could ever do! Shuts down all our ammo for digesting the disgusting lump of greasy stodge that you call food, and then we're even worse off than if you took nothing. You need *extra* hydrochloric acid, not *less*—not to mention digestive enzymes.

OS: Well—

Liver: So you can add ignorance to the long list of human shortcomings... How can you be so clueless and cavalier about your own bodies and expect things to keep working?

OS: You're getting a bit worked up—

Liver: You bet I am. Someone needs to.

OS: So, is there some way to get your message through to him?

Liver: Are you dense or something? You're it. You're my only chance. I wouldn't be wasting my time talking to you otherwise.

OS: But how can I—

Liver: Listen, the message has obviously got to come from the outside, unless I bring things to a head by crashing some of his systems.

OS: But—

Liver: I get it. You don't want to get involved. You're all the same—all in denial, all focused on your own stuff, too busy to be bothered by inconvenient truths.

OS: Hang on a sec. I didn't say that.

Liver: But it's true, isn't it?

OS: No. It's not. And you've got a very jaundiced view of humans.

Liver: Huh.

OS: So much for you being the seat of intuition.

Liver: What's the point of this cosy little chat, then?

OS: I felt it might be useful if people understood you better.

Liver: If you're so smart, how come you don't know about my emotional side?

OS: You have an emotional side?

Liver: Course I do. All the organs have an emotional aspect as well as a physical one.

OS: So what's yours?

Liver: Guess.

OS: A sense of injustice? Feeling hard done by?

Liver: Nah. That's the thyroid. Much further north.

OS: Something to do with conflict?

Liver: No! Adrenals!

OS: What, then? Just tell me!

Liver: I'm responsible for planning and creativity, and for instantaneous solutions or sudden insights. Part of my emotional brief is to help orchestrate things, get life running smoothly, and then ensure some payoff for all the hard work.

OS: Sounds good.

Liver: If things are running smoothly, I help generate kindness, benevolence, compassion and generosity. But rub me up the wrong way or take me for granted, and I get really angry, irritable, frustrated and resentful. If I don't get the cooperation, downtime or nutrients I need, I see red, and nasty stuff starts happening in relationships—jealousy, depression and other stuff.

OS: So if your man doesn't keep his liver healthy, you can't help him find that healthy balance and get the payoff or positive outcomes that he wants?

Liver: People have no idea how much their liver determines their mood, energy levels, health and outlook on life. I'm like the General, in charge of strategizing, and I help to generate order and meaning in life. Without my help, this guy will soon start to feel worn out by life, and deeply fatigued. He has to help me so I can help him.

OS: Makes sense, since you're sharing the same body.

Liver: Well, it would be better if he actually *wanted* to be healthy, rather than just going through the motions, at this late stage of the game, so he doesn't die.

OS: Yes. I—

Liver: Some appreciation would be nice, after all I've done.

OS: I get it. If he appreciated all the life-saving tasks you perform every day, he'd actually be happier.

Liver: He'd perform better, think more clearly, be more creative, have a sharper vision of his life, and be a lot more efficient with his time and energy.

OS: Makes no sense for him not to work with you on this.

Liver: If he works *with* me, he actively chooses to live, which creates a positive life force that's very magnetic. If he doesn't, he's choosing to die because he's making everyday choices that promote death versus life. It's a choice he's actively making, even if he does nothing. So he needs to ask himself this: *Am I a liver or a dier?*

25. Interview with an heirloom tomato
[bullying/self-acceptance]

OS: You're an amazing shape.

Tomato: Ugly, you mean.

OS: No—

Tomato: Deformed.

OS: N—

Tomato: Misshapen. Grotesque.

OS: No! I think you're fabulous—vibrant and unique, just as nature intended.

Tomato: I'm an original.

OS: Some people might consider you to be a bit misshapen. I'm guessing you see a lot of that.

Tomato: Yup. Had a buddy recently who was even more twisted-looking than me and he got beaten to a pulp.

OS: Oh.

Tomato: It's bullying, pure and simple. If you don't look 'normal' or the 'right' size, you get picked on.

OS: Unfortunately, it happens.

Tomato: Best case scenario, we get manhandled and end up all bruised, but some people even put us in boiling water to take off our skin.

OS: I guess they have trouble handling the skin...

Tomato: Skin, size, shape... These are your criteria for being acceptable? It's *your* sorry world that's flawed, not me.

OS: There are flaws, for sure—

Tomato: Most people want a nice, round, shiny, red tomato, with no 'imperfections', no strange-looking bits. They want uniformity and I'm certainly not part of that club.

OS: Yet it's your weird and wonderful shapes and colours that make you special and interesting. And, of course, you actually *taste* like a tomato.

Tomato: Yes, but you can't cut me into perfect round slices so I look nice on a plate. And appearances are everything.

OS: I think self-image matters far too much.

Tomato: All those fresh-food wannabes in the supermarket are what people find attractive. But they're just lookalikes, with none of the goodness found in the originals.

OS: I know. I always buy org—

Tomato: Imposters! It's a reflection of the times, I suppose. Same thing is happening with people.

OS: Not being real, you mean?

Tomato: How many people dare to show up authentically, warts and all? Everyone wants to fit in, be accepted, not stick out like a sore thumb. They all want to be the same nice, tidy size and shape.

OS: True. They're afraid of being rejected, of not being accepted for who they are.

Tomato: So they become something they're not and they get rejected anyway—and they're *more* likely to be picked on, teased, bullied, because of their insecurities. Which gets them even *more* bent out of shape. Great strategy.

OS: I don't think people see that, when they're feeling that way...

Tomato: Doesn't make sense. You all want to get noticed, be a success and beat the competition, yet you hide behind conformity and convention. Don't you realize that it's your quirky bits that make you interesting? Not being like everyone else is what gives you the competitive edge.

OS: We definitely need to foster greater acceptance and to weed out this bullying and abuse. It's been around for so long, handed down through generations...

Tomato: Hey, we've got our own stuff, handed down since the 1940s. But we're hanging in there, hoping for wider recognition of the priceless diversity we provide.

OS: So the genetic erosion that people talk about is a very real threat?

Tomato: We're genetically unique, with an evolved resistance to diseases and pests—apart from humans. If all us heirloom species die out, there'll be a lot more plant epidemics and infestations, putting your food supply seriously at risk.

OS: And all our natural resistance to disease is being killed off, too—through denatured food, as well as drugs, chemicals and pesticides.

Tomato: Being denatured seems to take you further away from being good-natured.

OS: Funny how those two things seem to be connected.

Tomato: So, which would *you* rather be remembered as: a rotten tomato or a priceless family heirloom?

26. Interview with an oak tree
[wisdom, being yourself]

OS: I'm absolutely fascinated by trees. I spend so much time looking up at you when I'm out walking that I have to be careful not to trip.

Oak: Well, we are pretty awesome. Oxygen, shade, fabulous shapes, ever-changing colours, natural beauty, wood, bark, leaves, mulch... what else gives so much and takes so little?

OS: I can't think of anything. And there's something powerful about all that vibrant greenery...

Oak: I don't think we'd look half as good if we were bright pink.

OS: No. Green is easy on the eyes and feels so healing.

Oak: Healing is just one of our many gifts to humans. We also foster wisdom, nobility, power and a sense of longevity. Try living for 200 years.

OS: I can't imagine lasting 100. I can't imagine a world without trees, either. It would be a desolate place.

Oak: It certainly wouldn't be a healthy place. Of course, it's already unhealthy, in many ways, but we counter a lot of the damage being done.

OS: But that's hardly your role.

Oak: Our role goes way beyond the physical and aesthetic.

OS: You have a spiritual aspect, too, right?

Oak: All of nature does. Back in the times of a more earth-based spirituality, our power was recognized and honored. We were even used by the Celts to access the psychic realms.

OS: And now people walk around with their cell phones, texting, never even looking at you... They don't know what they're missing.

Oak: Well, you know how much better you feel looking up at us, when you're walking, rather than staring down at your feet or at the lifeless cement.

OS: Uplifted, every time. You look majestic and so... *in charge* of your space.

Oak: Our roots run deep and wide. You can't reach for the skies if you're not properly grounded in the earth.

OS: I think we've lost that connection—living in high-rises, all stacked up on top of each other in compact little boxes, with layers of cement and other stuff between us and the ground.

Oak: If you don't stay connected to the earth, you're more susceptible to unhealthy forces.

OS: Such as?

Oak: All the radiation from all the fancy electronic gadgets and appliances you're so addicted to. Your bodies were never designed to deal with that kind of thing.

OS: Yet most people seem unaffected by it.

Oak: Might look that way, for a while, but you're electrical beings and any electrical charge passing through your body must be grounded so it doesn't build up and cause inflammation or disease.

OS: It's amazing we don't all have frizzy hair and electrifying handshakes.

Oak: Give it time...

OS: We'll never go back to the way things were. Technology is such an integral part of our lives.

Oak: Well, your only hope of staying healthy long term is to be grounded in the earth.

OS: You mean walking on the earth?

Oak: Yes, but walking barefoot. Not much point in trying to ground yourselves if you're wearing plastic- or rubber-soled shoes. Very little of the earth's energy can get through.

OS: None of the earth's *warnings* seem to be getting through, either. People just don't want to hear this stuff. It gets in the way of their fun.

Oak: Well, it will be interesting to see which of us you end up killing off first—yourselves or us.

OS: I think we need a more organic kind of growth, rather than focusing on technology, at the expense of other aspects.

Oak: What do you think would happen to me if I kept growing in just one direction?

OS: You'd keel over, obviously...

Oak: As technology takes you further and further away from your natural roots, you're going to see a whole new category of imbalances—and a lot more people are going to lose their minds.

OS: Their minds?

Oak: Yes. If there's too much electrical activity in the brain and not enough grounding, you'll fry your circuits. Humans need to engage in a lot more lateral, creative thinking if they ever hope to bring things back into balance.

OS: I've often wondered about your balance—how you manage to create such a perfect canopy and how you know where and when to branch out.

Oak: I reach for the sun—to get the maximum sunlight by expanding my reach in every direction. I can't understand why humans don't do the same.

OS: Reach for the sun? What would that look like?

Oak: Avoiding congestion and too much overlap. Finding a clear, open niche rather than competing with others. Seems like a natural way to operate for success, not to mention survival. For me, it's the only way.

OS: Makes sense. Your limbs and branches always look so evenly spread out, so your functionality is also a thing of beauty.

Oak: As all functionality should be. It's not enough for things to just work. They must work beautifully for all involved. If they don't, they're not really working.

OS: They're damaging something or someone...

Oak: Usually both.

OS: It certainly puts a different spin on success.

Oak: True success can only be measured in terms of how well it serves all living things. Anything that causes more damage than healthy growth is not success at all; it's exploitation. How long do you think trees would last if we all sucked up the earth's resources and gave nothing back?

OS: Not long. And that would affect us, too, of course.

Oak: Not that you ever think of that the other way around...

OS: No. We're incredibly self-centred. We think everything in nature is there to serve us. It's embarrassing.

Oak: Embarrassment, shame, guilt, regret ...it's all meaningless unless it prompts you to take some positive action.

OS: True.

Oak: So, how are you going to branch out?

OS: As a person?

Oak: As a creative force, an entity, someone with the ability to make a difference.

OS: Mmmm... I have a hard time figuring out the best way to do that.

Oak: I don't have to figure out how to be a tree, do I?

OS: No, but that's obvious.

Oak: And being you isn't?

OS: Not always...

Oak: That's where you need to create some growth—blossom, in some way. If you thought of it in terms of flowering or coming into full bloom, what might that look like?

OS: Well, getting properly grounded first, I suppose, since that's the key to growth and strength, right?

Oak: And what effect would that have?

OS: I'd spend more time reflecting, musing. I'd be more connected to myself, more in touch with my intuition, imagination and creativity.

Oak: Well, that's everything, right there.

OS: But I don't know where that would take me.

Oak: Of course you don't. That's the nature of creative growth. You can't possibly know where your next original thought or idea is going to take you—or where it's going to come from. And every creative choice you make takes you to a whole new set of options.

OS: It's totally unpredictable...

Oak: You think I know in advance which way every branch is going to twist or turn? It all depends on what's around me, how much sunshine there is, how firmly rooted I am and how rich and healthy my soil is.

OS: So we need to connect with what's around us, find a healthy supportive environment, eat nutrient-rich foods, seek openings for growth ...and remain as grounded as we possibly can?

Oak: How grounded I am will determine the extent of my reach, and how much impact I have.

OS: Yet we seem to be so hindered by our roots—by what we've been taught and by the environment we grew up in.

Oak: Your roots are not meant to determine who you become. They're just a launching pad, and where you go from there is up to you. Which is where your creativity comes in.

OS: In what way?

Oak: Your roots provide the push, your creativity provides the pull, and the conflict between the two creates a desire for solutions, betterment and release.

OS: Nice.

Oak: The more grounded you are, the more creative you can be.

OS: How come?

Oak: Because being truly creative requires courage, and courage comes from feeling safe, and feeling safe comes from being connected and solidly grounded within yourself.

OS: So we use our roots and our creativity to grow into the fullness of who we really are.

Oak: Mighty oaks from little acorns grow. And acorns, just like you, have innate intelligence that brings them all the growth they need.

OS: Mmmm... I'm trying to think of a quirky acronym for acorn, as a handy reminder for myself. *Awesome Creature Or Real Nutcase*?

Oak: That really doesn't do either of us justice, although it's clear to me which is which. What about this: *All Creativity Offers a Reflection of your Nature*.

27. Interview with a bar of dark chocolate
[addiction]

OS: This will have to be quick.

Chocolate: Oh?

OS: You're melting in my hand and I refuse to waste a single atom of my favourite chocolate. Plus, I've only got half a bar left.

Chocolate: Ah. You're one of those.

OS: One of what?

Chocolate: A chocoholic.

OS: Everyone loves chocolate, surely. [*I break off a big square and chew it slowly, eyes closed.*]

Chocolate: Yes, but just how *much* do you love it?

OS: Hang on. I never talk when eating chocolate... Just let me... oh, so good...

Chocolate: I think you may have just answered the question...

OS: What was the question, again? Oh, yeah. Well, you're the highlight of my day and everything else revolves around you. I only eat food so I can buffer the impact of the caffeine/sugar hit. Meals, work, socializing—they're all just a prelude to those luscious moments of melty, dark, rich, bittersweet magic. Can't see the point in anything else, without it.

Chocolate: Well, that means one of three things: there's not much else going on in your life or I'm exceptionally good chocolate.

OS: Lots going on in my life, but you *are* exceptionally good. What's the third thing?

Chocolate: You're seriously addicted.

OS: Dark chocolate's *good* for you! Everyone says that. What's wrong with having a nice little therapeutic dose of daily deliciousness?

Chocolate: Nothing wrong with it, but who are you kidding? You're not eating this for your health.

OS: Okay, okay, so I'm eating it because it tastes fabulous and it feels so good that it couldn't possibly be bad for me. Happy now?

Chocolate: Isn't that what smokers say about cigarettes?

OS: That's completely different. They're addicted to the nicotine and all that other nasty stuff.

Chocolate: And you don't think you're addicted?

OS: Course not. I gave it up for an entire year, once.

Chocolate: Classic addiction syndrome... What about now? Do you feel the need for chocolate?

OS: Yes, but only because of all the wonderful magnesium and antioxidants in it and the effect it has on that happiness stuff— serotonin. I'm probably deficient in those.

Chocolate: You're certainly deficient in something...

OS: Can't we just focus on the good stuff—your sensual seductiveness, how you boost endorphins and promote pleasure, well-being, positive mood?

Chocolate: Smooth. Nice deflection. You know, eating comfort foods is a mild form of addiction—and not always so mild, either.

OS: Yeah, so? What's that got to do with me? [*I break off another square and munch, quasi-orgasmically.*]

Chocolate: And all addiction is compensation for something, or a way to numb yourself from pain, stress or unwanted feelings.

OS: Glad we got that squared away. Can we move on?

Chocolate: So what do I help you to deal with—or *not* deal with?

OS: Me? You think I'm avoiding something or comforting myself by eating chocolate? Don't you realize that there are countless sad people roaming the planet, feeling as if something's missing in their lives, and they don't realize that it's *chocolate*??

Chocolate: Another nice deflection. But let's talk about pleasure, since you brought it up.

OS: What about it?

Chocolate: Do you realize how often you associate pleasure with pain?

OS: No pain, no gain. That's what they say. Wow, only one square left! How did *that* happen??

Chocolate: When you resort to comfort foods, alcohol or drugs, you're relying on a temporary external pleasure to mask a long-term internal pain. You're keeping that pain alive—buried alive. And you know what happens to things that are buried alive.

OS: Gosh, let me think...

Chocolate: If you addressed the pain, and went right into it instead of suppressing it, then your pleasure would be all the deeper and more meaningful—and I'm not just talking about your moments of choco-bliss.

OS: So you think I should give up all this life-affirming yumminess, allow the nasty, negative feelings to surface, and look forward to a richer, pain-free existence of choco-moderation?

Chocolate: Something like that.

OS: If I don't do it, am I going to live to regret it?

Chocolate: Well, I'm certainly not going to.

OS: What's next, then?

Chocolate: You're going to eat my words so you won't have to eat your own?

OS: Let me reflect on that a moment, while infusing my brain with the stimulating substances contained in this last square of divine deliciousness... Ahhh... That seems to have pumped up my brain power quite nicely. [*I crumple up the foil wrapper.*] Right, then, clarify this for me, so I know how to go about this monumental shift... [*But then I realize what I've done...*]

OS*:* Darn. Foiled again. Oh, well. I'll just have to interview another bar—and *then* I'll give it up...

28. Interview with Mary Angellica Iantha Makemgettit, channelling her spirit guides Voxir, Iki and Nebulosis
[integrity]

OS: Given our short time here on Earth, do you mind if I just call you Mary?

Mary: Oh, no, dear one. That's okay with us.

OS: Are you channelling this?

Mary: Let me just ask... [*She closes her eyes, sways back and forth...*] Yes, it seems I am.

OS: Don't you have your own answers?

Mary: Oh, yes, dear one, but there's so much wonderful divine information available to you all—

OS: Could you please dispense with the 'dear one'? And if you could switch channels, I'd really like to speak to Mary, on her own.

Mary: Oh. Okay.

OS: Now, I understand the value of being inspired by something outside ourselves—like Mozart, Rembrandt or other great artists or musicians have been. But why do you need to *channel* it—to attribute it to some other-worldly entity with a funny name, speaking in a funny voice?

Mary: Well, the divine spirits have a lot to share with us and it's a time of huge energy shifts on the planet, so—

OS: But surely whatever comes through you becomes yours.

Can't you just express it, own it and let it be you?

Mary: Well, the spirits want to help us and their words can have more impact when they're channelled directly.

OS: For many people, they have *less* impact. Channelling can be a real turn-off, especially if it's about trying to impress people or get more credibility for what you're saying.

Mary: People *love* my channelling. They can't wait for me to tune in and transmit wisdom that they wouldn't otherwise get.

OS: But isn't that a sign of insecurity—needing to channel some higher being in order to be taken seriously? And surely it's the height of spiritual arrogance to assume you can ever really know what's coming through you, where it's coming from and whether that source has a name or even exists.

Mary: You've obviously never experienced really good channelling.

OS: Actually, I have. I've had entire books come through me—but I'm happy to put my own name on them, since I was the one who actually wrote them.

Mary: That's a little different...

OS: Like many other intuitive practitioners, I also get insights and psychic 'hits' when working with clients, but I don't feel a need to claim that it's channelled information. We all have access to that kind of inspired wisdom.

Mary: The kind of privileged information we receive only comes through when we connect to the divine source and open ourselves up to receiving and transmitting it.

OS: Are you saying my information is not privileged?

Mary: No, just that it's not necessarily coming from the same place.

OS: But how can your source be better than mine if we're all one?

Mary: I think you're twisting my words.

OS: I'm just reflecting back how twisted they are.

Mary: I don't want to deal with this kind of resistance. Why should I?

OS: No reason, except that you're claiming to channel an authority that's higher than yourself.

Mary: What's wrong with that?

OS: Nothing, unless the information is wrong or out of integrity.

Mary: It's not me giving it. It's the spirits.

OS: Ah. That's handy. So you can blame them if someone doesn't like what you say?

Mary: That's ridiculous. They know things we don't and they can see things we can't see.

OS: But how do you know where you end and they begin?

Mary: Because I connect with them when I go into an altered state of consciousness.

OS: How do you know it's *them* when you're channelling and it's *you* the rest of the time? What if it's the other way around? Maybe you're only really you when you're in that altered state. How would you know?

Mary: I just *know*, that's all. I can feel it.

OS: Maybe it's you all the time but you're just in different states, accessing different parts of you, at different times. We do that all the time—when we meditate and even in our dreams.

Mary: I don't think so.

OS: You can't be 100% sure, though, can you.

Mary: I'm as sure as I am about anything.

OS: I guess certainty, like knowledge, is relative.

Mary: Sounds as if you don't trust anyone.

OS: I trust in the power of me and you. I trust in the power of human interaction to ignite our creativity and to reveal wisdom we didn't know we had.

Mary: I like that.

OS: Thanks. Plus, I trust in what feels right for me and I recognize the truth about myself when I hear it. What else do I need?

Mary: Others might know better.

OS: Oh, yeah? Like the Church knows what's best for Catholics?

Mary: Spirit guides might have information that could help you.

OS: I recently listened to someone channelling and they were telling their audience that they should purchase some products that the channeller just happened to be selling. Does that sound divinely inspired to you—not to mention *ethical*?

Mary: What's not ethical about it? If the information has value...

OS: Claiming to channel an authority that knows better than your audience and using that to sell your stuff. You don't find that just a tad unethical?

Mary: Like I said, if it's useful—

OS: So the end justifies the means? People in positions of power often invoke God when they want to enhance their credibility. Politicians do it all the time. And religious fanatics do it when they want to further their cause.

Mary: I think it's sad that you're not open to a source of divine intelligence that could really enrich your life.

OS: I'm very open to it and I tap into it every day. What makes you think I'm not open to it?

Mary: You're disputing everything I say.

OS: I'm questioning things that all of us should question. We're human, with massive egos and an aching need to be accepted and liked. We want to succeed and to have significance. But we're so deeply programmed that we can't always know our true motives.

Mary: So you can never really know anything.

OS: Exactly. But questioning the unknowable opens our minds to more expansive thinking and pushes us to know ourselves more deeply.

Mary: But spirit guides can help you to know yourself better.

OS: By telling me what to think? Anyone who does that, rather than encouraging me to tap into my own wisdom, is really not operating in my best interests.

Mary: You have a lot of resistance to being helped.

OS: Perhaps. But being helped and being told what to think are two different things.

Mary: So how *could* they help you?

OS: By helping me to see through the beliefs and programming that stop me from accessing my own answers. By challenging me to think in new ways. By supporting me in processing my emotions so that I know what I really feel.

Mary: They can certainly help with that.

OS: But so can you. You don't need them to help me with that. Do you?

Mary: Well, they can do it better. They have wisdom that I don't—

OS: I disagree. You don't need to *channel*, per se. You just need to stay connected to your own version of the truth. Channelling someone else diminishes you. You are it, and whatever comes through you is you.

Mary: My guides add value to what I already am.

OS: I've consulted many channels and as soon as they switch over to that 'higher authority', I sense that I've lost them. One minute they're sharing their own innate wisdom and intuitive insights; then, all of a sudden, they've switched into this stream of consciousness that doesn't feel right at all. Deep in my gut, I know it's off the mark.

Mary: Well, that's a pity. They're obviously not properly grounded or connected to spirit.

OS: Funny. That's what they all say.

Mary: Is there nothing I can say to convince you?

OS: Nope. The only thing that would enhance your credibility would be an admission of your humanness.

Mary: What do you mean?

OS: Admitting that we can only ever be right about some things, some of the time, for other people. You can't necessarily be right for me, but you can help me to be right for myself.

Mary: Okay... I'm certainly not always right...

OS: What about the higher authorities you channel? Can they be wrong, too?

Mary: In essence, no. But if I'm not really clear, I might distort their message, I suppose.

OS: Oh, so you are human, after all.

Mary: I never claimed to be perfect.

OS: No, just divinely connected, with access to privileged information, from an authority that knows more than ordinary mortals know.

Mary: I think we've been over this...

OS: It's our unquestioning deference to authority that feels unhealthy. It disconnects us from our own wisdom and clarity. It crushes our spirit and creates unhealthy dependencies. When we defer to others, we tend to switch off our minds and intuition, so we never get to explore what might be locked away inside. And if—

Mary: If you don't mind, I'd like to get on with the rest of my life.

OS: Gosh, sorry. I think I might have been channelling there, for a minute.

Mary: That's not funny.

OS: Don't Vox, Ik and Nebby have a sense of humour? Surely they must, with names like that. How can they possibly help humans if they don't? Maybe they're up there laughing themselves silly at how seriously we all take ourselves.

Mary: They have a sense of humour, but it's not necessarily *your* kind of humour.

OS: Not much use, then, is it.

Mary: You're very judgemental.

OS: I have opinions, just like them.

Mary: You sure do.

OS: Humour lightens us. And isn't this all about being

enlightened? Don't we need to laugh at ourselves, more than anything?

Mary: We certainly need to cultivate greater self-awareness.

OS: I think we need to acknowledge our own authority and to start trusting our ability to know what feels right. Turning to gurus, cults or religion is just a symptom of self-doubt, and depending on them makes us doubt ourselves even more.

Mary: I absolutely agree.

OS: Excellent. Well, now that we've clarified that, do you think your guides could give me some tips for promoting my next book?

29. Interview with a peanut
[authenticity]

OS: You've acquired some strange connotations: '*a paltry thing, a very small amount of money...*', among other things. Doesn't that make you feel insignificant?

Peanut: Not really, although it's hurtful, of course. But then I'm very aware of how easy it is to get lost in the crowd.

OS: How do you deal with that?

Peanut*:* I understand how difficult it can sometimes be to come out of your shell. I mean, look at what happens to me. As soon as I'm out of there, I get seriously roasted and a-salted.

OS: Yet that's when people love you the most!

Peanut: Funny, isn't it? But the prospect of exposing myself like that is daunting.

OS: What motivates you?

Peanut: Well, I know that if I stay in my shell for too long, I'll get stale and then no one will want me.

OS: So you force yourself to be strong and just go for it.

Peanut: It's all about showing up and getting involved. I need to get out there and mix with others.

OS: And what happens when you do that?

Peanut: Well, it can feel overwhelming when there are so many of us, but I try to get in with the right crowd—like a trail mix or maybe a party mix, depending on my mood.

OS: But not everyone really respects you, do they?

Peanut: Being called 'cheap' is one thing, but I've been called earthnut, monkey nut, pygmy nut, pig nut... And I'm not even a nut! I'm a legume.

OS: People can be very cruel, but those are just labels resulting from their ignorance. You mustn't let it get to you. You're so full of goodness!

Peanut: Yeah, but I'm easy to pick on because I'm so small.

OS: There's far too much of that going on, these days.

Peanut: Some people have very strong reactions to me. Can't stand me at all, in fact.

OS: Well, there will always be those people, I suppose. Doesn't mean that you're not well liked and appreciated by countless others, though.

Peanut: People rarely realize how multifaceted I am. They don't take the trouble to really get to know me.

OS: It's all about showing up and having a good profile, isn't it? Letting people know who you really are and what you're capable of.

Peanut: I'm not just a humble food, you know. I'm used as a fertilizer, I'm used to make paint, furniture polish, nitroglycerin—even soap and cosmetics. My proteins are used to make textile fibres and my shells are used in making plastic, wallboard, abrasives, paper and a load of other stuff. I'm even part of humanitarian projects to help starving nations.

OS: I had no idea.

Peanut: Yeah, well, like I said, most people don't bother to get to know me.

OS: Do you often get mistreated?

Peanut: Well, if I'm not handled properly or kept in a healthy environment, I can get an infection and give off toxins, and then nobody wants anything to do with me.

OS: Does that happen a lot?

Peanut: Not as much as before because there are laws against it now, but it still happens, although it doesn't always get reported.

OS: What happens when it does?

Peanut: If we have too many toxins, we get taken out of circulation.

OS: So you get rejected a lot?

Peanut: Yeah, well, being a peanut's not all it's cracked up to be, you know? Amazing as we are...

OS: Such a shame, given all your qualities.

Peanut: It's no fun living in the shade, I tell ya.

OS: What's the biggest payoff for coming out of your shell?

Peanut: Being made into peanut butter. Then we can blend right in and we seem much more acceptable that way.

OS: Well, it is very good... although there seem to be a few jokes out there about peanut butter.

Peanut: Don't even go there. I'm not telling you any because I know you'll only spread them around. I've shared a lot of personal stuff with you, about being shy and all that, so...

OS: Okay, no problem. Some jokes can be good, though, right? In Ireland, where I come from, we love to make jokes about people we really like.

Peanut: Yeah, right. Nice try.

OS: Any tips for other sensitive people who have difficulty coming out of their shell?

Peanut: You've got to let yourself go a little nuts. Be outrageous and don't let anyone tell you you're not up to snuff. Steep yourself in a supportive environment and allow your true nature to come out—like when you soak me in water overnight to break down certain enzyme inhibitors and make my goodness more bio-available.

OS: That's good advice.

Peanut: Hey, I may be small but I can pack a punch.

OS: Oh, yes.

Peanut: Not everyone will like you or even be able to handle you, but that doesn't mean you're not the best thing since sliced bread—with peanut butter on top.

OS: That's got to be the ultimate.

Peanut: I think all you shy, sensitive people out there should focus on your originality and quirkiness. Don't just strive to be acceptable and to blend in, like me. Don't even try to be the ultimate partner, colleague or boss. Take it to the hilt, and choose to be an *ulti-nut*.

30. Interview with a toilet
[denial, disowning]

OS: Oh, boy. I'm not sure I want to do this one.

Toilet: What—the interview? Or...

OS: Yes, the interview! Not... the other.

Toilet: Well, take a seat and let's talk about it. Lid down, please. I won't be able to concentrate, otherwise.

OS: Well, of *course*! [*I sit on the closed lid.*] This is not a topic most people want to talk about—and I'm not sure they'll want to read about it, either.

Toilet: Well, that's never stopped you before. In fact, isn't that what you love to do—be a shit-stirrer?

OS: Well, yes, but this is a lot of... um...

Toilet: A shitload of reality, is what it is.

OS: Exactly what people *don't* want, like I said.

Toilet: It's exactly what you're gonna give them, then. So let's just get on with it. Shit or get off the pot, right?

OS: Aghhh. Okay, okay. So... here's something I've always wondered about, although I seem to be in the minority: *Where does it all go*??

Toilet: All the shit, you mean?

OS: Yes! We flush it all down the toilet, wash our hands and get on with our lives. We never give it a second thought.

Toilet: And I make sure it all stays out of sight, with my nice curvy S-bend plumbing and auto-filling cistern

OS: Out of sight, out of mind—the wonderful American Standard. How can we be so *blasé* about something this important? Our cities are packed with high-rise buildings, with hundreds of people living in each one—all flushing their toilets. I can't imagine the tonnage of body waste that must be pouring out, every day, and going... *somewhere*. Where does it all *go?*

Toilet: Some of it gets treated, and some of it goes straight into the ocean.

OS: But it's *our* ocean—the source of the fish we eat, the seaweed we harvest... How can we be so short-sighted? How come this subject is not high on the political agenda when a mayor or politician is running for office?

Toilet: Yeah, right. I can see them doing a poll as part of their campaign: *How do you feel about this shitty issue:* a) *You care and you want to take action.* b) *You care and you want someone else to take action, through higher taxes.* c) *You just don't give a shit.* My guess would be (c), for most people.

OS: Yet there's so much talk about sustainability, values-based business and all that nice-sounding eco-friendly-speak, while tons of raw sewage are rushing by, right under our feet.

Toilet: People don't want to be bothered with that nasty, smelly stuff. They want their lives to be nice and clean.

OS: But aren't our ecosystems reaching their limit?

Toilet: Sure, just like your bodies are. You're doing just as much toxic dumping internally as you are into the environment. Same old micro–macro yada yada...

OS: People don't want to take responsibility for themselves, which means they won't take responsibility for their environment, either.

Toilet: Sometimes they're so busy dealing with the other shit in their lives that they can't face the shit inside—or the fact that they're actively poisoning the world in which they're so determined to have a good time, no matter what.

OS: You're quite articulate, for a toilet.

Toilet: Well, people do a lot of ruminating when they're sitting on me. They talk to themselves, they read out loud, they pour out all their problems. I feel like a hairdresser who can't talk back, but I learn a lot.

OS: But don't you think that taking personal responsibility for all our, um, shit would change everything? In some places, we now have special green bins for our organic food waste. Why can't there be something similar for our bodily waste? If we were forced to deal with *that* every day, how would that change things?

Toilet: Well, there'd be a lot more constipation, for one thing, but the pharmaceutical companies would love it. They'd probably come up with a new drug for composting your crap while it's still inside you, so that it came out all lovely and green, in tight little bales, smelling of citrus and ready for spreading on the lawn or growing your own vegetables. *Real* recycling, you might say—out one end, in the other, rather than the other way around.

OS: Hey, that's not a bad idea. They could call it Lax-U-lawn or Fibertilizer. And they could spread it on all those endless acres growing wheat and oats, rather than using the chemical stuff. Gives a whole new meaning to Crapola Granola.

Toilet*:* It would never work, though. There are too many toxins in your food. Your crap would be crap.

OS: The problem's at the other end, then.

Toilet: Isn't it always.

OS*:* Why IS that?

Toilet*:* If you paid more attention to what's coming out—*and* you had to deal with it, hands-on—you might be a bit more discerning about what you put *into* your system. You should see the stuff that comes out of people—

OS: Oh, no. Please don't...

Toilet: See? That's your problem, right there. You should all be able to talk about the shape, size and texture of your stools as readily and unselfconsciously as you talk about all the different coffee beans at your local café. You could have fun with it.

OS: Really?

Toilet: You could come up with all kinds of colourful, affectionate names and categories for the stuff: *Roasted Himalayan Yak Turds. French-roast Fatty Floaters. Double Espresso Sludge. Americano Inky-stinky-pooh. Super-pungent Rectal Resistors...* that kind of thing.

OS: What about *crappuccino*?

Toilet: Now you're talking! See how easy it is, once you get going?

OS: I'm thinkin' a cappuccino could actually *lead* to a crappuccino, with all that dairy congesting the system...

Toilet: You're right about that.

OS: Apart from the fun factor, though, what would be the point of getting all graphic about our bowel movements—our BMs...?

Toilet: Your poop is a very reliable indicator of your health— physical *and* emotional. And it's a great leveller...

OS: Ha. I can just imagine people going into the office in the morning and chatting with their employer. *Yo, boss, how were the shits, this morning? Backed up a bit? Oh, sorry to hear that. Must be those tight-assed company policies...* Guys could come up with some great chat-up lines for the secretaries: *Hey, babe, will you be my BM BFF?*

Toilet: Well, it would have to become the accepted norm, of course, which might take a while. But just imagine how things would be if you could all share at that level of raw honesty, without shame or guilt.

OS: Is that why there's so much constipation in our world—all that guilt and shame?

Toilet: Of course. Everyone's holding on, holding back, afraid to really let go and be themselves. Same reason they eat such crap, too—trying to make up for not feeling worthy, confident or lovable. Just how lovable would you all feel if other people could see what comes out of you?

OS: But maybe that's *why* it's not always nice or easy—we're so consternated, we're constipated, which causes all kinds of backlogs and unhealthy festering... rather than cleanly letting go of the past and, well, loving our shit as well as ourselves.

Toilet: The waste in your system has already been digested and processed—or *should* have been. If you can't let it go, it means you're holding onto a past that holds nothing good for you. You've already taken from it everything it can give you. Holding on creates toxic waste matter, which means you're poisoning yourselves with your past—your regrets, recriminations and missed opportunities. You can't be present, loving and powerful with all that stuff backing up inside you.

OS: Seems as if this kind of problem often needs to be in our face before we address it. Unless we get our noses rubbed in it, figuratively speaking, we'll just keep ignoring it.

Toilet: Forget the 'figuratively'. You've got to change your crappy attitude to this stuff. Your *crapitude* is killing you.

OS: But how *do* we change it?

Toilet: Reframe the way you view it. Think of SHIT as '*Simply Humanity In Transit*'. Life's just passing through you. But it's part of you, like the blood in your veins. You must love it and listen to it. Ignoring it means that you're flushing tons of valuable life-enhancing clues down the toilet.

OS: So it's a crucial indicator for what's going on inside.

Toilet: More than that, it holds huge potential—for you and for the planet. Think of CRAP as '*Creating Resources And Power*'. With the right mindset and technology, all that waste could be turned into fabulous, revenue-generating, clean fuels and fertilizers, among other things.

OS: So it's not dirty or shameful...

Toilet: ...unless you make it so, which you do. You disown it when it's *in* your body—like a fart (*It wasn't me!*). It's like saying: *That dreadful pong couldn't possibly have come from my pristine, well-cared-for, diligently-fed, pure body*. Right?

OS: I get it. What we're putting in is often as unhealthy as what we're ashamed of coming out.

Toilet: And you disown it when it's *out* of your body, sending it straight underground, into the sewers, out of sight. *Then* you disown it when the seas get fouled up.

OS: So we need to claim it back. We need to take ownership of it and make it a really good thing.

Toilet: It IS a really good thing—or can be, if you treat it right. It's only waste if you don't use it. And it's only toxic if you abuse it—or yourselves.

OS: Sounds as if we need a revolution—a whole new movement.

Toilet: Definitely. Best not to call it the Bowel Movement, though. Might put people off.

OS: Got any other suggestions, before we put the lid on this thing?

Toilet: It's obvious; you should call it FLUSH.

OS: What does that stand for—*Feeling Lucky... Until Shit Happens*?

Toilet: I was thinking more along the lines of: *Finding Life-enhancing Uses for Shit from Humans*.

31. Interview with a dandelion in seed

[freedom]

OS: I'd love to get your take on li—

Dandelion: Life is eeeeaaaasy!

OS: Okay, b—

Dandelion: Easy, peeeeeasy!

OS: Could I just a—

Dandelion: There's nothing to be done; it's all done for you!

OS: Look, I need to get some *substance*, here. This is an *interview*.

Dandelion: Substance?? Ain't gonna happen. *Look* at me! You see substance here?

OS: Well, no. I can see right through you, actually.

Dandelion: That's because of my wonderful transparency—something you *don't* get with humans.

OS: True. So, wha—

Dandelion: What you see is what you get. I just go with the flow, you know? *Pouff!* ...and I'm off ...wherever the wind takes me. I trust that and it never fails. You humans are far too hesitant, controlling, suspicious, fearful... You need to let *go*—like I do, when my seeds are ready to take flight.

OS: But what are your—

Dandelion: I'm *very* easy to impress.

OS: How come?

Dandelion: Haven't you seen how easy it is to blow me away??

OS: Ha. Right... What would you say are your best qualities?

Dandelion: I'm almost weightless—so light, so free!

OS: Free is good, but you don't last very long.

Dandelion: Well, how long have *you* ever felt this free for?

OS: Mmmm... good point.

Dandelion: I've got loads of good points, yet I'm pointless. Isn't that liberating?

OS: You're considered to be a weed—something people want to uproot as soon as you appear on their lawn... preferably before you go to seed and spread all over the place.

Dandelion: They just don't appreciate the difference between beauty and perfection.

OS: Which one are you?

Dandelion: Actually, I'm both, but they see me as a blot on the landscape—an imperfection—even though I'm quite beautiful, up close, when I flower. And I'm perfect in my own delicate, ephemeral way, when I go to seed ...like now.

OS: Yes, you are quite beaut—

Dandelion: I'm like a summer version of a snowflake. I'm a work of art—more delicate and intricate than a crystal vase. I'm like a spider web in 3D. I look spiritual, heavenly, ethereal. No wonder kids want to blow on me and make a wish.

OS: You talk a lot for something with so little substance.

Dandelion: Well, as you said, I don't last long, so I think it's only fair that I do all the talking.

OS: What message would you give to others, based on your experience?

Dandelion: People don't appreciate what's right in front of them. That's what being free *is*, after all—being absolutely present to what is and loving it. I mean, I love being here all the more because I could get blown away any sec— [*a gentle breeze lifts and the seeds start to slowly float away*]. Oh! Here goes... I'm off!

OS: That was quick... Well, thanks for talking with me—or at me... whatever. Darn. I didn't even have time to take a photo.

Dandelion: Photos can't capture all my angles and filigree wisps. Nothing can capture me... that's how free I am! [*Voice starts to fade.*] Floating, dispersing... can't ... down.

OS: Didn't catch that last bit. You're breaking up...

Dandelion: Duh... that's what dandelions *do* when their seeds disperse. Oh, you humans... always trying to control and contain things—to hold on to what no longer is...

OS: But—

Dandelion: See? Still holding on... Me? I'm already exploring new opportunities for my seeds to take root and grow. Get with the *flow*gram!

A note on subconscious programming and religion

The imaginary interviews in this book represent a creative romp through the deeper recesses of the mind, as well as a playful exploration of some of life's burning questions. In several of these conversations, the issue of subconscious programming is an underlying theme. I explore the power and purpose of our early subconscious programming in many of my blogs and other writings, which you can access via my website. Here, I would like to offer some insights into the value of testing and questioning your beliefs—*particularly* if millions of others believe the same thing.

Religion is one of the primary sources of negative programming in our lives, yet many of us accept its tenets unthinkingly, simply because they have been so deeply programmed into our psyche in our formative years. It can be a touchy topic and one that is often avoided because of its contentiousness. Even if we do not consider ourselves to be religious, many of our negative beliefs about ourselves and our world stem from early religious indoctrination. In asking questions that few dare to ask, in a realm that is all too often fraught with conflict, divisiveness and fanaticism, I like to break with convention and challenge widespread limiting beliefs.

Our beliefs usually become embedded in our subconscious minds from an early age—long before we can make up our own minds about anything. As adults, we rarely stop to objectively reconsider them or to make a fresh choice based on what feels right for us personally. (It would be extremely difficult for us to be objective, even if we wanted to be, given the pervasiveness of religious programming in all cultures and societies.) Because religious and other beliefs generally become rooted in us when we are forming our identity, they often feel deeply personal. For this reason, we may find ourselves taking offence if someone speaks negatively about 'our' religion, sensing a threat to our very foundation of self.

In reality, we are not *born* Catholic, Protestant, Hindu or anything else (although we are innately spiritual). We are born into families or societies that happen to practise certain religions, and we are raised in the context of those particular beliefs and values, which may or may not support us in being healthy, empowered human beings. Only by mindfully re-assessing them later in life can we hope to make them truly ours... or not, as the case may be. Without that critical discernment, they are simply beliefs that we have absorbed and allowed to remain unchallenged within us, affecting our performance, circumstances, relationships and self-worth.

In these interviews, I have allowed myself to have fun, unconstrained by convention, expectations or a fear of offending people—not because I don't care whether I offend or not, but because I know that caring too much about what people think cramps our style and hinders our personal evolution. It prevents us from asking probing questions, seeking a deeper truth, expressing our unique perspective, expanding our minds to include new possibilities, and going beyond the collective beliefs that often limit our lives.

Giving ourselves permission to explore things more honestly cultivates greater self-acceptance and emotional freedom. As an empowerment coach and counsellor specializing in human dynamics, I have witnessed the freedom that comes from questioning everything and figuring out how we operate, at the deepest possible level. In my 30 years of research and private practice, I've been fortunate to uncover some important pieces of the complex human puzzle. We are all innately worthy and powerful and, despite being shaped and often distorted by our upbringing (which sets us on our own unique evolutionary path), we are ultimately responsible for our own minds, beliefs and lives.

If you have suffered abuse in religious institutions, as so many have, or if you have 'merely' been programmed to not think for yourself, remember this: you have the right to not remain silent.

About the author

That would be me—Olga Sheean. I'm from Ireland ...which explains a lot, don't you think? The Irish love to laugh at themselves, and we've had to develop a healthy sense of humour to cope with all the rain and religious oppression. When I was growing up, many of my peers enjoyed getting legless at the pub on a Friday night. I never did fit in with that crowd, but I learnt a lot by observing people who drank to avoid their problems yet whose problems were exacerbated by too much drinking… and perhaps not quite enough deep thinking.

Things have changed for the better, since those early days, and I have many wise, alcohol-savvy Irish friends (and family members). Back then, though, not being a drinker of alcohol, or even black tea, I was more an objective observer of the Irish social scene than an active participant in it. It's no wonder, then, that I chose to specialize in human dynamics and behaviour, with so much rich material to study, in sober solitude.

Having lived in Canada, Belgium, France, Switzerland, New Zealand and several other nice warm countries, I've worked internationally as a mastery coach, relationship counsellor, writer, magazine/book editor, publisher and photo-journalist, specializing in relationships, human dynamics, creative potential, conscious evolution and general debunking of collectively pre-programmed conventional thinking.

My work and life are about exploring the deeper truth of our super-humanness and the nature of reality, maximizing performance, while enhancing leadership, creativity and magnetism—and having fun doing it. With a focus on transforming negative subconscious programming and achieving greater ease, success and fulfillment, I offer online consultations, empowerment intensives, relationship workshops, Dream Teams©, Life Changers© and online training.

I live with my artist–author–designer–marketing–magician husband, Lewis Evans, with whom I've developed numerous creative projects and far too many laugh lines.

For more information: https://olgasheean.com.

Look for these other titles
by Olga Sheean

available via her website: https://olgasheean.com/books

Fit for Love—find your self and your perfect mate

ISBN: 0-9738222-1-X

This fully illustrated guide to healthy relationship may be the most rewarding emotional fitness programme you ever undertake—one that will generate more breakthroughs and miracles than you could ever have thought possible. Filled with wisdom, exercises, practical techniques, full-colour illustrations and inspiring case histories, *Fit for Love* takes you on a journey of self-discovery, healing and empowerment, showing you how to access and transform the negative subconscious programming that has prevented you from fully accessing or expressing your true self. Through this book, you will gain an understanding of your powerful ability to create what you want, to enjoy lasting, healthy relationships, and to upgrade all aspects of your life.

A practical and insightful book that reveals how our relationships are powerful pathways to self-realization and personal fulfillment.

—John Kehoe, author of *Mind Power into the 21st Century*

The Alphabet of Powerful Existence—an A–Z guide to well-being, wisdom and worthiness

ISBN: 978-0-9879291-2-9

This practical guide to self-empowerment, featuring 52 themes (one for every week of the year) and offering simple, transformative steps for resolving conflict, positively reprogramming your mind, making powerful choices, and creating more love, money, ease, success and fulfillment in your life. Upgrade your relationships, finances and business; fill in your 'missing pieces'; activate your creativity; and enhance your self-worth and personal magnetism.

Olga Sheean brilliantly inspires us in practical ways to live a dynamic, healthy, fulfilling life on our terms. This book will enable you to change your circumstances, heal, and discover yourself. An enjoyable, easy read. I couldn't put it down!

—Bev Ogilvie, author of *ConnectZones: building connectedness in schools*

Gut Feelings—the inside story

ISBN: 978-0-9738222-3-6

A body odyssey with guts, attitude and a bellyful of laughs—a quirky off-the-wall story about the internal shenanigans of the body and the external dynamics of modern-day relationships. Nowhere else will you learn about lymphomaniacs, the *real* purpose of your appendix, or the spiritual significance of chocolate cake. This book is a madcap marathon through fact and fiction, adventure and enlightenment, mix-ups and makeovers, inside and out. The perfect gift for someone you love, or someone who doesn't get out much.

This book is a masterpiece—a humorous, all-encompassing, richly informative study of human beings that enlightens and educates the reader in a very digestible way. I recommend it for everyone over the age of 12. I also see it as a tool for teachers who are educating young adults on the challenging topics of health, self-responsibility and emotional well-being— topics that this book makes very accessible and fun.

—Aviva Roseman, MA (Young Adult Literature)

Tell Me The Truth—a code for freedom

ISBN: 978-0-9879291-5-0

This book is your antidote to the tsunami of commercial spin, social stimuli and bad news clogging our news channels and our consciousness. It challenges you to remember who you are and to change direction in favour of humanity and life. See the spin for what it is; let go of over-stimulation so you can reconnect with the real you; and trade the bad news for the good news and the truth about you and your world. Bad news and commercial spin promote fear and distort the truth, causing us to forget who we are. They misrepresent our quantum reality and disregard our creative capacity for change. The deeper truth is something else altogether. When we embody it, we find freedom.

This book is an uplifting meditation on life, written with extraordinary wisdom and insight. Not limited to any age, but a 'must' read for young people who stand at the crossroads of their lives, seeking answers, direction and fulfilment.

—Elize Potgieter, lecturer, Informatics and Design
Cape Peninsula University of Technology, Cape Town

EMF off! A call to consciousness in our misguidedly microwaved world

ISBN: 978-1-928103-10-3

A unique blend of wisdom, humour, personal experience, hard-hitting science and quantum physics, this book presents a compelling case for a complete rethink of how we live. Backed by an in-depth understanding of human dynamics, it explores the biological, psychological, neurological, emotional and environmental impacts of our insatiable hunger for wireless connectivity. Only by consciously engaging our neglected hearts and souls can we truly understand what is driving us and how we can become the game-changers of our own reality. This book provides practical steps for doing this, explaining how to activate our spiritual faculties and take ownership of our own lives.

Olga Sheean takes us on an intimate personal journey. Along the way, she challenges us to cultivate our deeper truth, reconnect and choose love. Our relationship with technology is like nothing our society has ever faced, and only we can cure our own addiction. I'm so thankful for this book.

—Theodora Scarato, MSW Executive Director, Environmental Health Trust

The Parents: How far would you go to save your world?

ISBN: 978-1-9281031-4-1

To create your own future, you sometimes have to completely rewrite your past. When Marnie, Matt and Lucy discover that their parents—both quantum physicists—have committed suicide, leaving no explanation and zero inheritance, it turns their lives upside down. Their parents were healthy and had everything to live for. Why would they do this? The answer lies in a strange past and an unimaginable future. An antidote to all the dystopian scenarios and depressing state of our world, with real solutions and a stonking good story, *The Parents* is a thriller with attitude, humour and conscience—a mind-bending read that takes you into the realms of impossibility and beyond. It will rock your world and draw you into an exciting new one—a world you won't want to leave and could create, if you choose…

A wish-it-were-true revolutionary sci-fi thriller that would make Nikola Tesla smile and send the rest of us on a transformational journey back to a world worth living in!
    —Roger Herried, clean-energy expert, co-founder of the US Green Party